"Maybe this would be a good time to tell you something," Tricia said, pulling away. "I'm a virgin."

Noah couldn't say anything. Think anything. He was shocked.

"I'm sorry," he finally said. "I don't know what to say." He ran his hand down her hair, but she pulled back, clearly hurt. "Tricia, this isn't the way to lose your virginity. On a couch in my office. We should have thought this through. I seem to lose control when I'm around you."

She looked at him. "I'm sorry, too, Noah. But you don't need to worry," she said, straightening her shoulders. "I won't let it happen again. It'll be back to business for both of us." She smiled in a way that said she was confident, but then faltered a bit.

"Back to business then. That would be best," he said finally. He hoped he had convinced her.

Convincing himself was another matter....

Dear Reader,

This book is the second in a trilogy about the Falcons: three brothers who rise above a chaotic childhood to become strong, capable, successful men by sheer force of will, and then become so much more when they find the right woman to love and be loved by.

It's also about understanding that nothing can be changed about our pasts except our perspective, which sometimes must be adjusted in order to get what we want in the present—a life that's richer, more rewarding and just plain fun. As my heroine says, "Life's short. Make it an adventure." Maybe we can't always control what happens to us, but we do have control over how we react to what life throws at us.

It's what I hope you take away from Noah and Tricia's story.

Susan Crosby

THE
SINGLE DAD'S
VIRGIN WIFE

SUSAN CROSBY

Silhouette®

SPECIAL EDITION®

Published by Silhouette Books

America's Publisher of Contemporary Romance

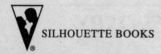

SILHOUETTE BOOKS

ISBN-13: 978-0-373-24930-5
ISBN-10:   0-373-24930-6

THE SINGLE DAD'S VIRGIN WIFE

Copyright © 2008 by Susan Bova Crosby

Visit Silhouette Books at www.eHarlequin.com

Printed in U.S.A.

Books by Susan Crosby

Silhouette Special Edition

*The Bachelor's Stand-In Wife #1912
**The Rancher's Surprise Marriage #1922
*The Single Dad's Virgin Wife #1930

Silhouette Desire

†Christmas Bonus, Strings Attached #1554
†Private Indiscretions #1570
†Hot Contact #1590
†Rules of Attraction #1647
†Heart of the Raven #1653
†Secrets of Paternity #1659
The Forbidden Twin #1717
Forced to the Altar #1733
Bound by the Baby #1797

*Wives for Hire
†Behind Closed Doors
**Back in Business

SUSAN CROSBY

believes in the value of setting goals, but also in the magic of making wishes, which often do come true—as long as she works hard enough. Along life's journey she's done a lot of the usual things—married, had children, attended college a little later than the average coed and earned a B.A. in English, then she dove off the deep end into a full-time writing career—a wish come true.

Susan enjoys writing about people who take a chance on love, sometimes against all odds. She loves warm, strong heroes and good-hearted, self-reliant heroines, and will always believe in happily ever after.

More can be learned about her at www.susancrosby.com.

To Renée Garcia, mom and home-school teacher
extraordinaire. Your value is beyond measure.
And to April Bastress, Education Specialist,
for the passion you bring to your valuable work.

Chapter One

Tricia McBride came to a quick stop a few feet from the interview room of At Your Service, a prestigious Sacramento domestic-and-clerical-help agency. She stared in disbelief at the owner, Denise Watson, who'd been filling her in on the details of a job opening.

"Hold on a second," Tricia said. "Let me get this straight. I'm not being interviewed by the person I would be working for, this Noah Falcon? I would be taking the job, boss unseen?"

"That sums it up," Denise replied. "It happens all the time, Tricia."

"It does?"

"Remember, I screen all my potential employers, just as I do my employees. If you find yourself in an impossible situation, you'll leave, but I don't think that'll be the case. Noah's a successful business owner, a widower with four children. Pillar of the community."

"Yet he's not doing the interviewing." Tricia didn't like how two and two were adding up. "There's something you're not telling me."

Denise hesitated. "Well, to be honest, he doesn't know his current employee is quitting. She told Noah's brother in confidence, and he decided to take matters into his own hands and do the hiring himself."

"Why's that?"

"You can ask him yourself." Denise opened the door, leaving Tricia no choice but to follow her inside.

An attractive man about her own age stood. Denise made the introductions. "Tricia McBride, this is David Falcon."

Greetings were exchanged, then Denise left them alone.

"Your résumé is impressive," David said, taking his seat at the conference table again.

It is? Tricia thought, but she said thank you then sat. "Why me, Mr. Falcon?"

He raised his brows at her directness. "Why not you, Ms. McBride?"

"I'm sure Denise told you I'll be leaving Sacramento in January to move to San Diego to start a new job. I would be in your brother's employ less than three months. That seems unfair to the family."

"And you're absolutely committed to this other job?"

"Yes, absolutely, unequivocally. I've given my word."

"Just checking," he said with a smile. "You know, it's obviously not the ideal situation for us. But the important thing is that we'll have that three-month cushion to find someone perfect, someone who *will* stay. Who knows, it could happen next week, and you'd be on your way. We're not guaranteeing the job for the whole three months, either. But in the past Noah has been forced into making expedient choices. You'll be giving him the luxury of time to find just the right person."

"By that you mean he loses employees frequently?"

David hesitated. "My brother tends to hire people fresh out of college who don't have a clue about life yet, not to mention how to handle four children. You were a kindergarten teacher, which leads me to believe that you like children, certainly a necessity for the job, plus you have actual experience working with them. You're thirty-four, so you have life skills, as well. Denise has done a thorough background check on you, and I feel comfortable that you'll be an asset."

She eyed him directly, not easily fooled. "And what's the real reason you're doing this behind his back?"

He half smiled. "Truth? Noah's children are in need of a woman like you, even if it's only for a few months. Their mother died three years ago. The house is…quiet. They need laughter. And someone who will stand toe-to-toe with Noah."

"Why?"

"He needs help, but he usually resists suggestions. Noah is still grieving. He doesn't know how to deal with his children."

"*Deal* with them?"

"Wrong word, I guess. He loves them. He just doesn't know how to show it."

He sounded to Tricia like a man out of his element and on the edge. "When Denise called me yesterday to talk about the job she made it seem like a nanny position, but after the details she gave me today, I'd say it's beyond that."

"It's more teacher than nanny. The kids are homeschooled, so your teaching background is important."

"Homeschooling four children is a far cry from being a nanny."

"Which is why the salary is so high. But the kids are bright and eager to learn."

"How old are they?"

"The boys are nine and the girls are twelve."

"Twins? As in two sets?"

He gave her a dry, apologetic smile. "Which is the other reason the salary is high. Yes, two sets of twins, who aren't nearly as intimidating as you might imagine. Just the idea of them tends to scare off the prospective help, which is why I asked Denise not to mention it."

"I'm really not sure about this…."

"I understand your reservations, but if you'll just give it a chance…" He leaned forward. "Denise is good at what she does, finding the right person for the job. In fact, she's down-right uncanny at it. Why don't I just take you to Noah's house now, while he's at the office? You can meet the children and see the environment."

The children. Tricia pictured them, sad, and lonely for a father who didn't know how to show he loved them. She blew out a breath, trying to dispatch the heart-tugging image. "Where does he live?"

"About an hour's drive north of Sacramento, a little town called Chance City, although not within the town itself."

"You mean it's in the *country?*" Tricia couldn't contain her horror at the idea. She'd spent her entire life in the city. She liked concrete and grocery stores and fast-food restaurants.

"Depends on what you mean by country. It's in the Sierra foothills," David said. "His home is large and comfortable, on ten acres of property."

"As in no neighbors for ten acres?" This was getting worse and worse.

"Or thereabouts."

"So, I'd have to live in? What about my house? I'm getting it ready to put on the market."

"You could get Saturdays and Sundays off. He can hire weekend help locally, if he wants to," David said.

Silence blanketed the room. Living in, with weekends off. Not exactly what she'd signed up for. Or expected. Then again, it was only for three months, and her mantra of the past year kept repeating in her head: *Life is short. Make it an adventure.* She just needed to keep her usual safety net in place, too.

"Okay," she said at last. "Let's go check it out."

Claws of tension dug into Noah Falcon's shoulders as he turned into his driveway and followed it to the back of his property. He drove into the garage, shut off the engine and sat, trying to shift out of work mode and into parent mode. The demands of owning a company were a breeze compared to being with his children each night. Somehow during the past three years they'd become almost strangers to each other.

Lately he'd found himself coming home later and later, knowing they would be ready for bed, if not already asleep, thus avoiding contact beyond a query about how their day had gone and what they'd learned. When he did manage to make it home for dinner, he tried to carry on a conversation at the table, but unless he continually asked questions, they were almost silent. He didn't know how to breach that silence, to get them to open up on their own.

And this was Friday, which meant another whole weekend with them.

At least tonight he didn't have to worry about what to do, since it was past their bedtime. But as he walked toward the house he saw his daughters' bedroom light on and realized he'd come home too early, after all. The rest of the second-floor rooms visible from the back side of the house were dark—the master suite and the bedroom the boys shared. Although there was a bedroom for each child, both sets of twins remained doubled up, choosing not to be separated.

He understood their need to be together and hadn't pushed them to split up, even though he remembered having to share with his middle brother, Gideon, when they were young, and begging to have his own space, not getting it until he was a teenager.

But twins were different. Closer. At least *his* twins were. And Adam and Zach were only nine, so they probably wouldn't be ready for individual rooms for a while yet. Maybe Ashley and Zoe never would.

Noah let himself into the kitchen through the back door. As usual, a plastic-wrap-covered dinner plate was in the refrigerator, along with instructions on how long to heat it in the microwave. He peered through the clear wrap and saw meat loaf, mashed potatoes and green beans. His stomach growled. He shoved the plate into the microwave, set it and headed upstairs to say good-night.

As he neared the landing he heard a woman speaking, her voice dramatic. The girls must be watching a movie, because it wasn't their nanny, Jessica.

He'd almost reached the doorway to the girls' room when he spotted all four of his children reflected in Ashley's floor-to-ceiling ballet mirror on the bedroom wall. They wore pajamas. The boys were nestled in beanbag chairs they'd dragged into the room from their own. The girls were lying on their stomachs on Ashley's bed, chins resting on their hands. All of them were focused on a woman standing off to the side a little, an open book in her hand.

She was tall. He was six-four, and he figured she was five-ten, maybe taller. Her hair was a wild mass of golden-blond curls that bounced as she dramatized the story. She used a different voice for each character and put her whole body into the performance—her whole very nice body. Blue jeans clung to long legs; her breasts strained against a form-fitting sweater. Incredible breasts.

She would look magnificent naked, like some kind of Amazon. A warrior woman—

Noah scattered the image. She was a stranger in his house, in his children's bedroom. Who the hell was she? And where was Jessica?

He moved into the room. The children turned and stared but said nothing, just looked back and forth between the woman and him.

"Good evening," he said to them.

"Good evening, Father," they answered almost in unison.

He saw the woman frown for a moment, then she came forward, her hand out. Brilliant green eyes took his measure. "Hi. You must be Noah Falcon. I'm Tricia McBride, your new schoolmarm."

Chapter Two

"My new...schoolmarm?" he repeated as he shook her hand. "But, where's Jessica?"

"Watching television in her bedroom. We can do an official changing of the guard on Monday." Tricia leaned close to him, sympathetic to his shock. "You need to call your brother David."

His mouth hardened. "In the meantime, may I speak to you in the hall?" he said, more a command than question, then he left the room without waiting for a response.

Tricia steeled herself for the discussion. She'd expected surprise and resistance, based on David's comments, as well as Jessica's. But having spent the afternoon and evening with his children, she'd decided she would make him hire her. They needed her. Period.

She set down the book and smiled at the children. "I'll be back to finish it with you. Why don't you have a pillow fight or something in the meantime?" She grinned as they looked at each other in astonishment.

She crashed straight into her new boss as she left the room.

"What took you so long?" he asked.

"Ten seconds is long? I was assuring your children that I'd be back to finish reading the story."

"Aren't they kind of old for bedtime stories? They do know how to read."

She was definitely going to have more problems with the father than the children. And, really, someone should've told her how incredibly attractive the man was, with his rich dark brown hair and eyes, and all that height and broad chest and shoulders. Too bad he didn't have a funny bone.

"Personally, I still love a good bedtime story," she said, realizing he was waiting for her to answer.

He shoved his hands in his pockets. "I take it Jessica is quitting."

"That's the scoop."

"And my brother found out and intervened and hired you."

"Yes. I imagine he's waiting to hear from you."

"Oh, he'll hear from me, all right."

She wouldn't want to be on the other end of *that* call.

"What's your background?" he asked.

"Kindergarten teacher." She figured he didn't need to know yet that she hadn't taught for five years. "Jessica showed me the curriculum. It looks doable." Just needed a little shaking up to add some fun to the program.

He angled away from her. "I'm going to talk to Jessica, then call David. Please come to my office when you're done reading to the children. Do you know where it is?"

"Jessica gave me a tour." Seven bedrooms, seven bathrooms, three stories. The tour lasted half an hour.

"Good." He started to walk away.

"I'm sorry. I must have interrupted your saying good-night to your children," she said cheerfully.

He gave her a long look then sidestepped around her and went back into the room. She followed, wanting to watch them interact.

No pillow fight going on, but that wasn't a surprise.

"So. Another change," Noah said, standing in the middle of the room between the boys and girls. "I'm sorry."

"It's okay," Ashley said with a smile.

"No, it's not okay," Noah said after a long moment. "I'll fix it."

The girls were sitting cross-legged on the bed. He ruffled their long, strawberry-blond hair and said good-night, then did the same with the boys, who were so similar in coloring to their father, dark hair and eyes. They each said, "Good night, Father," in return. He nodded at Tricia as he left the room.

She picked up the book again. She only had three pages remaining to finish the story and figured he would need some time to take care of his business. She started reading, noted that the children got caught up in the story again instantly, their expressions rapt.

Ashley applauded at the end. She was easy to distinguish from her twin, Zoe, because Ashley almost always smiled, while Zoe rarely did.

"I guess it's time for bed?" Tricia asked them, thinking it was early for twelve-year-olds, but they didn't complain.

The boys grabbed their beanbag chairs and headed for the door.

"I'll come say good-night," she said to them.

They looked at each other. "Why?" Adam asked. Tricia had noticed that Adam often spoke for Zachary, too, after exchanging a look. But Adam and his sister Zoe were also similar in that they were constantly moving. Even if they were sitting, their feet were rarely still.

"Because I like to," Tricia said to Adam. "I think it's a nice way to end the day."

Again the boys looked at each other. The overly quiet Zachary shrugged and left. Adam followed.

"You'll be here on Monday, right?" Ashley asked as she climbed under her blankets.

"Your dad will make the final decision, but I sure hope so. I'm looking forward to it."

"Why?" Zoe asked from her side of the room.

Zoe was easily the most intense of the four, the one to question why.

"Because I like you," Tricia answered.

"You don't even know us," Zoe scoffed.

Ah, yes. Definitely not one to just go along. "That's true, Zoe. And you don't know me yet, either, but I really like what I've seen already." She tucked Ashley's blankets around her. "Good night. Sleep tight."

Ashley clung to Tricia's arms for a moment, smiling sweetly. Zoe was resistant to being tucked in, so Tricia didn't try.

"Do you leave your door open or closed?" she asked. She'd already noted a nightlight on in their adjoining bathroom.

"Closed," Ashley said, quickly adding, "but not the bathroom door."

The slight tremor in her voice told Tricia all she needed to know. "Okay. Good night."

She went down the hall to the boys' room. The door was already shut, no slit of light under it. She smiled. They had a lot to learn about Tricia McBride.

She knocked. No answer. She opened the door wide, letting the hall light guide her way. Neither boy spoke. The lumps in their beds remained motionless. In the dark she couldn't differentiate between the boys and didn't know which one slept in which bed, either. She took her cue from what surrounded them. One side of the room was military neat. The other was a maze of sports equipment. She headed there first, tripping over a basketball.

"Good night, Adam," she said, rubbing his shoulder for a second. He lifted his head in a hurry.

"How'd you know it was me?"

"You are one of a kind, young man."

A moment of silence, then, "I am?"

"You sure are. Sleep tight."

"Will you be coming back?"

"I hope so."

She moved to Zachary's bed and repeated her good-night and quick touch to his shoulder. He didn't say anything until she'd reached the door.

"I don't remember your name," he said in the darkness.

"Tricia McBride. 'Night."

After shutting the door, she leaned against it for a moment, grateful she'd been able to tell them apart, hoping that impressed them in some way.

Then she headed downstairs to beard the lion in his den.

Noah drummed his fingers on his desktop, phone to his ear, as he listened to his brother defend his decision to do the hiring this time around.

"Doesn't hurt that she's easy on the eyes, either," David said, a wink in his voice.

"That's about the dumbest thing you've said. I've never gotten involved with an employee, nor do I intend to start."

"You should take a page out of my book. Worked for me."

"You took a huge risk by getting involved with your housekeeper. She could've quit, or filed a lawsuit, or—"

"Get engaged to me," David interrupted. "Turned out great."

"You were lucky."

"Damn straight."

"I didn't mean it in a good way, David."

David laughed. Noah settled into his chair. Actually, he was glad not to have to deal with interviewing and hiring yet another nanny, but he didn't want David to think he had free rein to interfere.

"The kids seem to like her," Noah said. "They've had to adapt way too many times. I hope this one sticks."

David was quiet for a few seconds, then, "That's my hope, as well."

Noah heard someone coming down the stairs and assumed it was Tricia. "I have to go. We'll talk more at the office on Monday."

"I guess I can wait until then for my thank-you gift."

Noah shook his head as he hung up. David wanted everyone to be as happy as he was, now that he'd found the right woman. Noah had already found and married the right woman, once upon a time.

A knock came at his door. "It's Tricia," she announced.

"Come in." He tried to take in her tall, curvy body again without her noticing his interest. Easy on the eyes, indeed, he thought, remembering David's comment. He indicated the chair across from his desk.

"They're all tucked in," she said, crossing her legs, her foot bouncing. "They are sweethearts."

He leaned back. "Thanks. It's been hard on them since losing their mother."

"I'm sure it has. That was three years ago, right?"

"Right, but don't give me any pop psychology about how they should be over it by now." He was so damn tired of hearing that.

Her foot stopped bouncing. "In some ways it gets even tougher as time goes by. They're probably not able to bring up her face so easily now, and I imagine that bothers them a lot. It's scary when the images fade, and you want so much to keep them near."

Her observation struck home hard with him. He was going through the same thing, even with pictures as reminders. He couldn't hear Margie's voice anymore, except that Ashley and Zoe laughed like her. "You sound like you've had experience with it yourself."

"My father died when I was eleven, so I do understand their loss."

He appreciated that she had that in common with the children. It could only help.

"Shall we discuss the job?" she asked. "Did David fill you in on me?"

"He said you want weekends off and would live in during the week. Cora, the woman who cooks and cleans for us, also only works Monday through Friday. That leaves me without anyone on the weekend."

She smiled in a way that said she wasn't biting. "Since you don't need the house cleaned or the children schooled on the weekend, you only have to feed and play with them. I assume they make their own beds? And you must be able to cook by now."

Apparently she was going to be difficult. "Is there a particular reason why you can't live here full time?"

Her brows went up. "Do I have the job description wrong? David said I was mostly to be your children's teacher. That's a Monday through Friday job, as far as I'm concerned. And everyone is entitled to time off, you know."

"The rather lucrative salary I pay," he said, "has always included the general care of the children. A nanny as much as a teacher. That means weekends, too."

"Then you'll have to cut my salary proportionately, because I don't want to live here 24/7. I live in Sacramento. Is there some reason why you can't parent your children on the weekend?"

She'd touched a nerve. He was already aware he was failing as a father. He didn't need someone who didn't know anything about him or his history telling him that, too. "Sometimes I have work to do," he said.

SUSAN CROSBY   21

"Then we're at an impasse. If you can't watch your children yourself, you'll need to hire weekend help. David must have told you I'm fixing up my mother's house to sell it." She cocked her head. "And I don't mean to be presumptuous, but you seem to be in a good position financially. You could hire a full-time, live-in staff."

"I haven't always been in that position. It's made me careful. Too careful, David tells me. I do what I feel is right for me, my family and my business." He had children to provide for now and in the future. He also had employees who depended on him, on the business he brought in and the solvency of the company. He lived up to his own personal standards, was proud that he did.

"Father?"

All four of his children stood in the doorway, crammed shoulder to shoulder.

"What are you doing out of bed?" Noah asked.

Ashley took a step into the room, her hands clasped. The others huddled around her. "We want Miss Tricia to be our new teacher."

He leaned back and steepled his fingers in front of his mouth. "I see. Well, I can't say for sure yet that she will be. Miss Tricia and I are still in negotiations."

"What's that mean?" Adam piped up.

"It means we're trying to figure out what would work best for all of us."

"The best is for her to live here," Zach stated, his voice quiet but strong.

Silence filled the room as the least talkative of the bunch announced his wishes.

"You just need to pay her a lot of money," Ashley said.

"It's not about the money," Tricia said, looking pleased at the children's insistence. "Your father pays a very good salary. The issue is that I need weekends off."

The children all looked at each other. Ashley seemed to take a silent vote. "We're not little kids anymore, Father. We don't need to have a nanny all the time."

"I'll take it into consideration. Right now you all need to go back to bed and let us discuss it."

Zach went up to Tricia and shook her hand, one big up-and-down shake, his expression serious. Adam followed suit, grinning.

Zoe came next. "Do you know how to play soccer?"

"I sure do."

"Okay." Zoe stuck out her hand for a shake, then left the room bouncing an imaginary ball from knee to knee.

Ashley finally approached. "Please say yes, Miss Tricia," she said, then gave Tricia a quick hug before she hurried out.

Noah saw how the children affected her. If she could become that attached after just a few hours, she was definitely the right one for the job. It would be a great weight lifted from his shoulders, too.

"So," Noah said after a long, quiet moment. "Saturday morning to Sunday evening off. And you'll be here this Sunday night."

She smiled. "Jessica's not leaving until Monday."

"Jessica will be gone by Sunday afternoon."

"I see." Tricia nodded. "Is five o'clock okay with you, Mr. Falcon?"

He stood. "Noah. And yes, that's fine."

She stood, as well. "I'm curious why you don't send them to public school."

"I made a promise that I would continue what my late wife started." He paused. "I'll walk you to your car. Where is your car, by the way?"

"Next to your garage. You didn't notice it?"

"I was preoccupied. Let me go tell the children that you've agreed to take the job. They won't go to sleep until they know. I'll be back in just a couple of minutes." He extended his hand, as his children had. "Thank you."

"I'm very happy we came to an agreement."

Her handshake was firm, one sign of her character. She seemed straightforward. She obviously could and would speak her mind.

The Falcon household was about to change.

As Tricia stepped outside with Noah ten minutes later, the chilly late October evening cooled her warm face and cleared her eyes and mind.

So. It was official. She was employed. She would have enough money to tide her over until she started her new job.

Peace settled over her at the thought, then the quiet around her struck her. Country life. It was going to take some getting used to. No. A *lot* of getting used to. But she was probably noticing the quiet even more because Noah hadn't spoken since they'd left the house.

"Have your children always called you Father?" she asked.

"Yes. Why?"

"You just don't hear it much these days. Did you call your father that?"

"No. Most of the time I called him a son of a bitch."

Tricia stumbled. He reached for her, caught her. She grabbed hold, steadying herself, then looked at his face, as he held her upright by her arms. At odds with the coldness in his eyes, his hands were warm, his heat leeching through her sweater. "Thank you," she said quietly, sorry when he let go. There was something comforting about his large and gentle hands. "Your words caught me off guard."

"No sense hiding the truth. I made it my goal to live as differently from him as possible."

"And you called him Dad, so you don't want your kids to call you that?"

They'd reached her SUV. She pressed the alarm button to unlock it.

"You haven't been here long enough to criticize," he said coolly. "Or analyze. I grew up in total chaos. It's not what I want for my children."

She opened her car door, wanting to escape. He was right. She should mind her own business. "I apologize, Noah. I was just curious. Everything seems kind of formal between you and your children." She didn't add what she wanted to—that they were all distant from him, physically and emotionally. And that they were starving for his affection. *Anyone's* affection, which was probably why they'd latched on to her so easily.

"Is there anything you'll need to start the job?" he asked, very directly changing the subject.

She sensed in him deep, unrelenting pain, and she wondered if he would ever break through it to embrace life again. Or maybe he never had. She shouldn't presume what she didn't know. Maybe she could carefully ask other people how he was before his wife died.

"If I think of something, I'll let you know or just go ahead and buy it in Sacramento," she said, getting into the car and sliding the key into the ignition. "I'll review their classroom work Sunday night so that I'm ready to go on Monday."

"You have my phone numbers?"

"Yes, thank you." She started the engine then glanced up at him as he rested an arm on the top of her door and leaned toward her a little. He really was an extraordinarily attractive man, even tightly wound as he was. She wanted to tell him that things would get better, that his life was going to change, that she would see to it, especially for his children. But did he want to hear that?

"Do you space out often?" he asked, his voice laced with surprising humor. "Should I worry for my children's safety?"

Her eyes were dry from not blinking. "You won't regret that your brother hired me," she said, wondering if it was true.

"David may have done the prelims, but I hired you. And my children. If any one of us had objected, you wouldn't be coming back."

"Of course," she said, then shifted into reverse. "Until Sunday."

He backed away, but he was still standing in the driveway when she looked in her rearview mirror before she turned onto the road. Maybe she'd been lying when she'd told him he wouldn't regret hiring her, because he may well be sorry. She was pretty sure she was different from any other teacher he'd hired before.

And she knew he was different from any boss she'd had.

Chapter Three

Standing in the kitchen, Noah watched his children say goodbye to Jessica, who had been their nanny for several months. Usually a changing of the guard, as Tricia had called it, was cause for moping and silent recrimination from the kids, but not this time. This time they said their goodbyes and let her leave, rather than following her outside to wave to her as her car pulled away.

They always liked their nannies. That was never the issue. The problem was that the nannies didn't usually like *him*. It hadn't been any different with Jessica, apparently, although she'd never indicated any problem before quitting. Even then she'd told his brother, not him, that she was leaving.

Noah knew he had a problem dealing with his help. He'd been giving it a lot of thought the past couple of days, analyzing the situation, trying to figure out how not to lose another nan—teacher. He should get used to calling Tricia that, since she seemed to prefer it.

He wondered why none of the other nannies had said anything about the job title. Maybe because they'd just graduated from college and hadn't taught in a classroom yet. He liked that Tricia had classroom experience. If she could handle twenty kids at one time, she must be able to handle four. Especially four, quiet, easygoing, uniformly bright children.

Not that he was biased or anything….

Margie would've liked her. Probably would've been a little intimidated by her, too, but his late wife would've liked Tricia's easy way with the kids and her refusal to back down—something he wasn't sure *he* liked. He was used to being in charge, at work and at home. There was room for only one boss in any situation. He didn't tolerate clashes of authority.

"She's gone," Adam announced, looking out the window as the car disappeared, then he glanced at Noah. "When will Miss Tricia be here, Father?"

Father jarred Noah now, since Tricia had brought it up. "She said five o'clock."

Which meant he had to figure out what to do with his children until then. Well, technically after then, too, since she wouldn't be on the clock. He hadn't even planned dinner.

He realized all four children were watching him, waiting. "Did you have something to say?" he asked, his gaze sweeping across them then landing on Ashley.

"We would like to have a family meeting," she said, her expression serious.

He shifted into head-of-the-family mode. "All right. Why don't we go into the family room?"

Their footsteps sounded behind him, seeming loud in their conversation-free trek. Even Adam was quiet, a rarity.

Noah sat in what was considered his chair, an oversize lounger that faced the television he rarely had time to watch. Each child took his or her usual seat on the sofa and other chairs.

"What's on your mind?" he asked the room at large.

"We think it's time for some changes around here," Ashley answered, all business.

"What kind of changes?"

"We counted up the nannies we've had. Seven."

That many? He knew there'd been a lot. And that didn't include his mother-in-law coming to stay for the first few months after Margie died.

"We're kind of tired of figuring out someone new all the time," Ashley said.

"I understand that. What do you think can be done about it?"

"We think you should smile more," she said without smiling.

"Smile more?" he repeated, confused.

"Not at us, Father. At Miss Tricia. Miss Jessica was scared of you."

Scared? Really? He liked order but was surprised he was feared. "I'll try," he said, adding it to his mental list of things to be aware of if he didn't want to lose Tricia as an employee. "What else?"

Ashley continued. "We want Miss Tricia to eat dinner with us, not in her room like Miss Jessica and the others."

Noah was fascinated with this new, mature daughter of his. "Why?"

"Because we think if she feels like she's part of our family, she'll be happier."

"You like her that much?"

"She seems okay. We just don't want another change."

"Yes, I know you're tired of it all."

Her hands folded in her lap, Ashley sat up a little straighter. "We also don't think you should argue with Miss Tricia about anything."

An improvisation, he decided, trying not to smile. "I can't

guarantee that. We are bound to disagree on some things. And you are *my* children, not hers. I know what's best for you."

They all looked at each other. Had they always done that or was it something recent? They seemed to be more attuned than before. Each set of twins shared a connection that had always been obvious, but not in combination with the other set. He figured they must be desperate, to face him like this, presenting a united front.

"Then please be nice *and* smile at her when you argue," Zach said, fixing Noah with a stare.

Laughter rose inside his chest. He couldn't let it escape or they wouldn't believe he was taking their concerns seriously. "I'll be nice."

"Thank you."

Noah leaned his arms on his thighs and looked at each of them until they each looked back. "Now. Is there something you'd like different for yourselves, not for Miss Tricia?"

Zoe raised her hand. "I want a swimming pool."

"Basketball court," Adam added.

Noah did smile then. How easily their focus changed. "Nice try."

Zach jumped out of his chair and raced to the window at the sound of a car coming down the driveway. "She's— Nope. It's Uncle David."

"Alone?"

"No. Valerie and Hannah, too."

Three of the children raced off to greet their uncle, his fiancée and her eight-year-old daughter, Hannah. Ashley lingered, moving more slowly with Noah toward the kitchen.

"Something else on your mind?" he asked.

She shrugged.

"Talk to me," he said, stopping just outside the kitchen door, his hand on her arm to keep her there, too.

"Can we watch the videos of Mom again sometime soon?"

"You know where they are. You're welcome to watch them anytime."

"I mean as a family."

He didn't know if he wanted to bring back all that pain. He'd stopped watching the videos when he realized they hurt more than helped. "Do the others want to watch, too?"

"Not Zach."

Which didn't surprise Noah. Zach kept the most inside.

"Okay. We'll do it tonight."

"Not tonight," she said in a hurry as the kitchen door opened and everyone came in, talking and laughing. "I'll tell you when, okay?"

"Sure." He was grateful for the reprieve.

Suddenly the kitchen teemed with people, then the kids all took off upstairs with their cousin-to-be Hannah in tow.

"We brought dinner," Valerie said, as David set a covered casserole in the oven and a bowl in the refrigerator.

"I chauffeured. *Valerie* brought dinner," David said. "She made everything."

"Thanks," Noah said, surprised. "But why?"

"To welcome your new nanny," Valerie said.

"Teacher," he corrected, looking over David's head to try to see what was in the bowl, guessing it was salad. David had lucked out when he'd hired Valerie through At Your Service. She was the calm, competent woman Noah had been looking for, too. He didn't think that description applied to Tricia. Well, competent, maybe. But calm? Probably not. *Lively.* That was a better word. "I hope you're staying for dinner, too," Noah said.

David made clucking sounds.

"What's that for?" Noah asked. "I'm not a chicken."

"You don't want to make small talk with your help."

"So? I've never liked to. It's no different with Tricia."

David stood. "She's just your type."

"She's on the other side of the world from being my type."

"Leave him alone," Valerie said to her fiancé, slipping her hand into his, firing a heat-seeking caution look with her eyes. "Yes, we'll stay for dinner. That was our goal, although David was supposed to call and alert you. I want to meet Tricia myself. I expect we'll become friends."

"She's here!" came a shout from upstairs, followed by the rush of footfalls scurrying down the staircase. As a group they ran through the kitchen and out the back door, Hannah grinning as she came last—following just to follow, Noah supposed.

"That's quite a reception," David commented, wandering to the window to watch.

Noah went to take a look. Ashley and Zach got up close to her. Tricia hugged Ashley, her face alight with pleasure, and said something to Zach that caused him to smile then look down at the ground. Adam and Zoe didn't allow her close enough to hug. She held out a hand to Hannah, an outgoing, happy girl who was just as caught up in Tricia's arrival as the rest of them.

Tricia opened the back of her SUV and started passing things to each child, then they marched toward the house like safari porters, carrying bags, boxes and garments on hangers, with Tricia bringing up the rear with the largest box.

"Aren't either of you big, strong men going to help her?" Valerie asked as the back door flew open and the children tramped through.

Criticized into action, Noah met Tricia at the back door and took the box from her.

"A welcoming committee. How fun," she said. "Hi, Noah. I'm glad to see you again, David."

"I'm more glad to see you," he said with a grin. "Tricia McBride, this is my fiancée, Valerie Sinclair."

The women shook hands. "Hannah must be yours. She looks just like you. She's darling."

"Thank you, yes, she's mine."

"They brought dinner," Noah said, balancing the box on the edge of the counter.

"Oh, how nice of you. And since you're not running off, would you mind if I excuse myself for a few minutes and go make sure the children haven't just heaped all my clothes on the floor?"

David and Valerie encouraged Tricia to go.

"Be right back," Noah said, then trailed her up the stairs. As he eyed her from behind he started to rethink the idea of putting in a pool, as Zoe requested. Getting a chance to see the teacher in a skimpy bikini—

"Maybe you should just come up beside me," Tricia said, stopping and turning around.

He kept his expression blank. Okay, she'd caught him. He was a healthy male who'd been without female companionship for three years. So sue him for admiring her very sexy body.

"I got it!" a child yelled from down the hall.

"I brought it up here!"

"I think the troops need a mediator," Noah said, hiding his surprise at the fact any of them were yelling, something that almost never happened. They all got along eerily well.

Tricia's mouth tightened, but she continued up the stairs again, and he allowed himself the pleasure of watching her hips sway until they reached the landing.

She stopped there instead of heading toward the yelling down the hall. "Do we need to have a discussion?" she asked him.

"About what?"

"Appropriate employer/employee behavior."

"I'm familiar with the laws," he said. "But why do you ask?"

"You know why."

"Enlighten me." He figured she was only speculating that he'd been eyeing her rear as she climbed the stairs. He'd painted her into a corner. Either she had an accusation to make or she didn't.

"I'm telling Father!" Zoe came charging out of the room. "Ashley won't let anyone help."

Noah moved past Tricia and Zoe. When he reached Tricia's bedroom, he set the box on the floor and looked around. The closet door was open. Clothes hung neatly on the racks, with shoes lined up like little soldiers on the floor below. Ashley and Adam were elbowing each other trying to put books onto shelves. Zach was perched on the bed, thumbing through a photo album. Hannah sat cross-legged on the floor, out of the way, wide-eyed. As an only child, she hadn't been exposed to sibling rivalry.

The tension was abnormally high, each child intending to make Tricia feel at home, but being pushy about it.

"Miss Tricia can put away her own things, and, in fact, probably prefers to. Everybody out," Noah said.

"But thank you for your help," Tricia added from the doorway.

Zach hadn't lifted his head. Noah slid the photo album out of his son's hands and pointed toward the door. Before Noah closed the album, he caught a glimpse of a photo of Tricia and a man wearing an army uniform, their arms around each other. She looked young and in love.

He set the album on the dresser. "I apologize for my children," he said to her. "They're trying to help. Obviously they went a little overboard."

"It's no problem."

"It is as far as I'm concerned."

She waited a beat. "You're the boss."

He remembered how Zach had told him to be nice, and how Ashley said he needed to smile. He wasn't doing what he'd promised his children he would. And none of them could afford to lose Tricia.

"I apologize," he said, purposely relaxing his shoulders,

trying to seem more accessible. "I wanted them to be on their best behavior for you. All of us, actually. Myself included."

"Why?"

"It's your first day. We didn't want to scare you off."

She laughed. Her face lit up when she smiled. Green eyes sparkled. "I'm not easily intimidated."

"Good. Is the room okay? Big enough?"

"It's beautiful. Since my time here will be limited, it'll do just fine." She hitched a thumb toward the door. "The children have put most of my things away, so we can get back to your guests. How long has your brother been engaged?" she asked as they left the room.

"Less than a week. He hired Valerie through At Your Service as his housekeeper and administrative assistant about two months ago. He's also adopting her daughter."

"How nice for all of them."

"Yes."

She cocked her head. "I hear a *but*...."

Should he voice his concerns out loud to someone he barely knew? Would she keep quiet about his reservations or tell David? Something about her invited trust. "They haven't known each other long, that's all. And David has said forever he wouldn't get married, so it's hard to feel comfortable about his decision."

They'd almost reached the bottom of the stairs. Tricia leaned close to say, "But they're just engaged, right? They'll have more time before the wedding to learn more about each other. They could change their minds."

He'd been prepared to hear her say the opposite—something about him being too jaded, or not a romantic or something. Instead she'd seen his point about how little David and Valerie knew about each other. He liked that she seemed practical.

He also liked how her hair smelled....

"We've been waiting for you," David said as they came into

the kitchen, a hubbub of conversation. Everyone held a glass of something pale and bubbly. David passed Noah and Tricia champagne flutes. Noah assumed the children's flutes held sparkling cider.

"What's going on?" Noah asked.

"I'm making a toast." David lifted his glass toward Valerie. "To my beautiful bride-to-be—for agreeing to marry me, and for not making me wait. You're all invited to our wedding, two weeks from yesterday."

Chapter Four

Tricia exchanged a look with Noah as they sipped the celebratory champagne. After a moment, he shrugged, apparently accepting the inevitable. She decided to make it a point to get to know Valerie and see for herself that Noah could relax about the quick marriage. She considered herself a pretty good judge of character.

Valerie shooed the men and children off to the family room while dinner was reheated.

"It's a good thing they're not depending on me to cook," Tricia said as Valerie opened a couple of loaves of buttered sourdough bread and put them on a baking sheet.

"You don't enjoy it?"

"My mom and I opened cans exceptionally well. And I make a mean PB and J sandwich." She smiled at Valerie, who smiled back.

"The reverse is true for me. My mother was a housekeeper

and cook for a family in Palm Springs," Valerie said. "She taught me everything."

"Does Hannah cook?"

"She's not quite as into it as I was, but yes. But, you know, I couldn't do what you do, Tricia. Teachers amaze me." She gestured to a cupboard. "Plates are up there."

Tricia grabbed plates, salad bowls, glasses and silverware and carried them into the dining room. "Tablecloth or place mats?" she called out to Valerie.

"Take your pick. They're in the hutch."

As Tricia set the table, she could hear the men and children playing video games in the family room. "They're having a good time," she said to Valerie, who was grating fresh parmesan cheese. Tricia leaned against the kitchen counter. "Can I ask you some questions about Noah?"

"You can ask, but I don't know a whole lot. I haven't spent much time around him."

"Do you know if he's always so serious?"

"I think I can safely say yes to that. According to David, Noah's a workaholic. He never takes a vacation. He's pretty much in charge and in control at all times. Doesn't have a great deal of patience. Very action oriented. And he doesn't like change."

"Yet I heard he's had a whole lot of nannies for the children. That's change."

"That's where the lack of patience comes in, I think. The whole interviewing and hiring process is too tedious, so he takes the quickest route."

"Does he date?"

"Not that I've heard." Valerie had just taken the salad out of the refrigerator and set it on the counter. She half smiled at Tricia. "These Falcon men are hard to resist, aren't they?"

Tricia straightened. "What do you mean?"

Valerie peeked around the doorway, making sure they

were alone. "I started falling for David the first day I worked for him, too."

"'Too'? Oh, no. Not me. Uh-uh." Tricia held up both hands. "I'm out of here in three months."

Valerie frowned. "What do you mean?"

"I'm temporary. David hired me to buy time for Noah to find someone who *will* be permanent."

"Does Noah know that?"

"I'm sure David told him." And she'd mentioned she was selling her house, and that her room here was fine for the short term. He hadn't flinched at either point. "So, tell me. What's this about you falling for David on the first day?"

"I didn't want to, but there it was. He makes me very happy. My daughter, too."

"Why the rush to get married?"

Valerie took out the fragrant, bubbling lasagna and slid the bread under the broiler. Almost immediately the pungent scent of garlic filled the air. "Why wait? It's right, and we both know it. Plus I won't move into his bedroom until we're married. I want to set a good example."

"You mean, you haven't slept together?" Tricia couldn't keep the surprise out of her voice.

Valerie laughed. "Well…David often works from home. And Hannah does go off to school."

"Oh. Okay. Good."

"Good?"

Tricia nodded. "I'll tell you why some other time."

"I hope you'll come to the wedding."

"I'm not going to be here on the weekends."

"Make an exception, please? I don't have many girlfriends here. I'd like for us to become that. I'll introduce you to my friend Dixie, too. She's my maid of honor. You'll love her. And there's the bachelorette party, of course. You have to come to that." She poured dressing on the salad. "Maybe you could tell the gang that dinner's on? I'm sure it'll take them five minutes to actually get to the table."

Tricia stopped just outside the family room door and observed the activity. Noah sat with his back to her, watching David and Adam play a video game, complete with hoots and hollers and threats of maiming. Ashley and Hannah were intent on a second television, but Tricia couldn't see the screen, so she didn't know what held their interest. Zoe bounced a soccer ball from knee to knee, not an indoor activity, but Noah wasn't objecting, which seemed odd.

Then there was Zach, who sat cross-legged at his father's feet, not communicating with any of them, but taking in everything.

He spotted her and smiled. She smiled back. "Dinner is served," she said to the room at large.

"You're doomed!" Adam shouted to his uncle, who shouted back, "Not yet, I'm not!"

Noah got up. Ashley stood right away, too, and turned off the television. She and Hannah made their way to the door, grabbing Zoe by the arm and pulling her along. Zach held back, putting himself between Tricia and Noah.

"Dinner smells *good*," Zach said.

"Looks like your uncle got himself a chef in the bargain. Do you like lasagna, Zach?" Tricia asked.

He nodded.

"We eat a lot of pasta dishes and casseroles," Noah said. "It's an easy thing for Cora to fix that will keep and reheat well. Sometimes my other brother, Gideon, comes over on the weekend and we barbecue."

They came into the dining room. It was obvious Noah sat at the head of the table, with David at the other end for tonight. Zach found his place farther down. Which left one empty seat, next to Noah.

Tricia expected at least a small amount of chaos with so many people, but it was all very…civilized. As an only child, Tricia had craved the noisy family dinner table she observed at some friends' houses. Here there were five children and four adults and little conversation. David asked questions, and the children answered, but no one took it further.

After the dishes were done, Tricia excused herself to put away her things and then to look over the children's past work. The third-floor classroom was huge. Each child had a desk. A computer workstation held two computers, but only one was connected to the Internet and was password protected so that the children couldn't log on privately. Areas were set aside for art and music, and worktables for science projects or other messier tasks. The room was tidy and spotless.

The view was spectacular, as the room was made up almost entirely of windows that faced the surrounding woodlands, and no neighbors in sight.

After a while, Ashley came up the stairs, dressed in her pajamas.

"We're going to bed," she said. "If you'd like to say good-night," she added hesitantly.

"Yes, I would, thank you." She put an arm around the girl's shoulders and walked down the stairs with her. "I'm looking forward to starting class tomorrow. Do you enjoy your schooling?"

"Sometimes. It kind of depends on the teacher."

"I'll do my best to make it interesting and fun, Ashley."

"I know you will," she said with a smile as they walked into her bedroom. Zoe emerged from the bathroom, her strawberry-blond hair damp and tousled, a dab of toothpaste above her lip. She hopped right into bed and pulled the blankets up to her nose.

"What time do you get up in the morning?" Tricia asked Zoe.

"When Ashley pulls the covers off and won't let me have them back."

Tricia smiled. "Who wakes you up?" she asked Ashley.

"My head. I wake up early on my own around seven. Then I wake up everyone else. We go to the classroom at eight. Zoe's usually the last one there."

"Do you make your own breakfast?" Tricia knew that Cora didn't come until eleven-thirty.

"I don't like breakfast," Zoe said. "It makes me sick to my stomach."

Ashley rolled her eyes. "We eat cereal or peanut butter on toast. And a banana or apple. We fix our own."

"What time does your father leave for work?"

"He's gone before we get up." Ashley climbed into bed and settled the bedding over her.

Tricia leaned down for a hug from her, then moved on to Zoe, whose body language said, "Don't come too close," so Tricia just smoothed back her hair and said good-night.

She encountered the same situation with the boys. Adam hugged her. Zack retreated from contact. She wondered where Noah was. She couldn't hear any sounds within the house.

How did he spend his evenings? Working? Watching television? Should she track him down and find out?

She decided to return to the classroom and finish reviewing the children's previous work. Thank goodness none of them were in high school yet and taking chemistry or something else she hadn't studied in years.

After a while she heard someone coming up the stairs, the footsteps heavy enough to be only Noah's. He called her name, alerting her that he was about to enter the room.

"How's it going?" he asked, standing at the top of the staircase, his hands shoved into his pockets.

She leaned back in her chair. "I'm making headway. At least it's early in the school year. They seem to stick to a fairly rigid schedule."

"That's my preference."

So, it *was* his doing that the children's class work was so highly structured. "I'll make an appointment to see their— What is the title of the person who oversees the children's schooling?"

"Educational Specialist, but everyone calls her an E.S. Cynthia Madras is her name."

"Thanks. I've read the rules and regulations on homeschooling, but I'd like her input on the children individually."

He dragged a chair closer to her desk and sat. "She'll tell you that Ashley is a visual learner who studies more than the others and worries if she doesn't do very well on tests. Zoe and Adam are kinetic learners who have a hard time sitting still and like to have a noisy environment, which drives Ashley crazy. And Zach is an auditory learner with an exceptional memory. He studies the least and absorbs the most."

Tricia liked that he knew so much about his children's learning styles. "I appreciate the summary."

"I keep a close watch on their education. I meet with each of them individually every evening to—" He stopped, hesitated. "I *used* to meet with each of them. I've been working so late the past year that I haven't gotten home in time most nights to have one-on-one time with them."

"So, you're not home for dinner?"

"Rarely."

"I see. Well, maybe you'll be able to incorporate the individual time into your schedule again soon."

"Maybe."

A long pause ensued. She knew she needed to change the subject. "Who cleans up the dishes at night?"

"No one. Cora takes care of it when she comes in."

"Do the children have any chores to do?"

"School is their job."

She decided not to start an argument with him on the value of responsibility through chores. Not yet, anyway. "Your future sister-in-law and I had a nice talk," she said instead.

He was obviously happy about the change in subject, because his expression smoothed out. "What do you think?"

"I think Valerie is head over heels about your brother, and yet very down to earth. I like her a lot. I expect I'll learn even more about her when I attend her bachelorette party."

His brows went up. "I'm sure you will. I guess as his best man I need to figure out a bachelor-party plan myself."

"Definitely. Next weekend. You don't want to have the party the night before the wedding. Saturday night, since Friday is Halloween."

"Right." He stood. "You're all set here, then?"

"Yes, thanks." A little nervous, but excited. "Are you ever gone overnight? For work," she added, realizing he might think she was wondering if he had a girlfriend or someone he visited when he had…needs.

"Not for the past few years."

"Good."

"Why?"

"I've always lived in the city. Being so isolated out here is kind of creeping me out."

He watched her for a few long seconds. "Come with me," he said, then he went down the stairs.

She followed because he gave her no choice. He waited at the foot of the last staircase, then they walked into the dining room, through the kitchen, into the utility room. He grabbed two jackets from the rack there, passed one to her, then he held the door open. She went down the stairs, putting on the jacket as she went. *His* jacket; she could tell from how the cuffs hung past her fingers.

The night was quiet and dark. Moonless. She couldn't see

the lights of another house or building, just stars. Millions of stars. She hadn't paid attention to them Friday night, hadn't paid attention to anything but him, and how he talked about his father.

Gravel crunched beneath their feet as they walked down the driveway to the four-car garage. She'd seen him drive a fancy black sports car, but had no idea of the brand. She figured it was his commute car. A large SUV was also parked in the building, a Cadillac.

"I'll give you a garage door opener," he said. "You can park in the garage. I want you to use the Caddy to drive the kids around."

"Okay." She tugged her collar up against her neck. "I don't even know what you do for a living, except that you and David are in business together."

"We own Falcon Motorcars, custom-made automobiles. We've been strongly in the European market for a long time but are moving more toward American business now. It's a big transition for us—David's brainchild, so that he can stay stateside more."

"So that shiny sports car you drive is one of your own?"

"The latest model. At this point we only produce the two-seater sports car, a four-door sedan, and made-to-spec limos. I'd like to incorporate an SUV, but that'll be a few years down the road, I think. We're headed to the American LeMans circuit first."

"You'll be making race cars?"

He nodded, then cocked his head as they heard a noise. "That's an owl."

"I'm not a complete idiot," she said with a smile. "What else is around?"

"Deer. Dogs and cats, wild and tame. Raccoons, fox, skunks, all the usual small wild animals. A variety of birds. Early in the morning you can sit at the kitchen table and see quail. There are grouse and mourning doves and hawks. None of them is your enemy, Tricia, although the deer eat the vegetation, which is annoying sometimes. And if threatened, any animal will protect itself. You really shouldn't worry about them."

At the moment she wasn't worried at all, because he was there with her. But on her own? She really, really hated the great outdoors.

"Is that why you don't have a garden?" she asked. "Because of the deer?"

He glanced toward the open space. "We used to have a garden. It was Margie's thing. She was into organics."

"Margie is your late wife?"

"Yes."

"How long were you married?"

"Eleven years. We met in college."

"You were happy," she said, hearing it in his voice, even layered with grief.

"Yes. Very."

"How did she die?"

"Pancreatic cancer. Very quick. Very painful."

His brief answers indicated he was done talking about it. "I'm so sorry."

"Thanks." He touched the small of Tricia's back, urging her toward the house.

That touch, that single, glancing touch through the layers of the jacket, rattled her. She was already worried about falling in love with the children and not wanting to leave in January. She didn't want to be worried about falling for the father, too.

It's just hormones, she decided. Long-repressed hormones coming out of years of hibernation, something she'd been hoping would happen—just not with her boss.

Inside the house, she slipped out of the jacket before he could help her, not wanting his fingers to accidentally graze her skin.

"Any questions?" he asked as they moved through the rooms to the staircase.

"Am I free to call you at work if I have any problems? Even ones that aren't an emergency?"

"Of course. My assistant's name is Mae. She'll know to put you through. Better yet, just call my cell. I'll always answer if it's you."

"Okay. I think that's all for now. We'll probably have things to talk about tomorrow. I would appreciate your letting me know if you're joining us for dinner, so I know whether or not to wait for you."

He looked annoyed. "I have business in many time zones. Sometimes I have to stay late for a call. I'll try to be here. That's all I can say."

Based on what David had told her, and on her own observations so far, Tricia knew Noah did his best to avoid being at home. That needed to change. "Your children miss you, Noah."

He looked about to fire back then smiled instead. Sort of. As if someone was making him. "I will try," he said quietly but resolutely. The boss, after all.

She didn't like his answer, but took it no further. However, she wouldn't hesitate in a week to remind him again of his responsibility to his children.

Tricia waited to be dismissed. Since she hadn't held this kind of position before, she wasn't sure of protocol, but she figured he would be the one to end the discussion.

"All your questions are answered?" he asked.

"For now."

"Then I'll say good-night. I hope you'll be happy here, Tricia."

"I'm sure we'll have a lot of fun together. The children and I, I mean."

"I know you're used to kindergarteners, who mostly just play."

"Please don't insult me," she responded. "You won't find their education lacking because of my teaching skills."

"I didn't mean—" He stopped, took a step back. "Good night."

As she climbed the stairs, she watched him walk toward his

office. Sympathy rose inside her. For all that he was successful in his work and had four beautiful children, he was not a
happy man. And not just because he still grieved for his wife,
she decided. Maybe he'd never been happy. Obviously his
childhood hadn't been good, his father no kind of role model,
although Noah didn't seem to be anything like his own father.

Tricia shut her bedroom door and leaned against it. She was
in a tough spot. Three months to help them as a family—
because that had become her primary goal now that she'd met
them—and still be able to walk away.

Get out now, she told herself.

The shouting in her head got louder and louder. She should
heed it. She knew she should. But superimposed over it were
the faces of the children, who needed her.

And Noah. Who perhaps needed her even more.

Life's short. Make it an adventure. Her brand-new mantra
began shouting even louder, reminding her of her own needs,
which she'd promised herself she wouldn't forget. *She* was
entitled, too.

But for the moment, she needed to be here, with this family.

Having an adventure.

Chapter Five

Noah pulled into the driveway the next night at six-thirty. He hadn't called when he left the office, and he could've called from his cell phone at any time, yet he hadn't.

He didn't know why. He wasn't rude, generally. Oblivious, maybe at times, but not intentionally rude. And it hadn't slipped his mind, because *she* hadn't slipped his mind. Tricia. He hadn't even been working, but reading trade magazines so that he wouldn't get home until a half hour after the usual dinnertime, although it was two hours earlier than his norm for the past year.

If he really wanted to figure out why he'd deliberately stalled, he could call his brother Gideon, who wasn't a psychologist but understood human nature better than most people.

Noah didn't want to know why.

He made the long walk from the garage to the house. No one opened the back door to greet him, although the dining room lights were on, and they all would've seen his car turn into the driveway, his headlights arcing across the window. Maybe they were done eating.

Margie would have had the kids racing to the back door to greet him.

He reached for the door handle, then stopped and reminded himself that his world had changed forever. There was no Margie. No wife. Even though the At Your Service agency where David had found Tricia was nicknamed "Wives for Hire," Tricia wasn't his wife. Except she was doing an admirable job of filling many of Margie's roles....

But no sex, of course. That was in the contract they both signed, although he wouldn't have gotten involved with an employee, anyway. It hadn't been an issue with any of the other nannies, contract or not. Tricia was the first one to even tempt him.

Noah entered the kitchen just as they were carrying their dirty dishes in, Ashley leading the way. Accusation and disappointment hit him full force from her expression alone. Why? He hadn't made it home on time for at least a year.

"Hi," he said, setting his briefcase on the counter.

"Hello." She turned on the faucet and rinsed her plate. She opened the dishwasher and slid her dishes inside then left the room.

"Dinner was good," Adam said. He put his dishes in the dishwasher without rinsing.

Zoe followed suit. "Beef stew," she said in way of greeting.

Then Zach, whose expression was even more accusatory than Ashley's. Why? What had he done?

Zach took his time rinsing his plate, using a cloth to get every bit off the plate and silverware, then loaded them. Finally he looked at Noah. "You promised to be nice," he said, then left.

Ah. So part of being nice was being home for dinner. Okay. Noah understood now.

"Hello, Noah. Did you have a good day?" Tricia said as she brought her own dishes in.

He was not in the mood to be chastised, directly or indirectly, and her tone indicated she was doing exactly that. He was especially annoyed because she'd been intruding into his thoughts all day already. "This is your doing, I assume."

"My *doing?*" She rinsed her dishes, avoiding looking at him. "Your children seemed to think things were going to change. I have no idea what or why. All I know is, you didn't call to say you were on your way home, so we ate without you. What's wrong with that?"

"I meant having the children doing dishes."

She looked startled. "*That's* what you're mad about?"

No. He was angry that his children were barely speaking to him, but he couldn't blame Tricia for that. "I don't want them doing chores."

"Why not?" She propped a hip against the counter and crossed her arms.

"Because you only get to be kids once."

"Home is where we are prepared for life. Doing chores is part of life."

"Not in my house."

"Noah," she said quietly, "the children want chores. They want responsibility."

"How do you know that?"

"They told me."

He didn't know what to say to that. He'd only meant to save them from the kind of childhood he'd had—babysitting his two younger brothers while his father and one stepmother, then another, worked full time. He was ten years old when he was first put in charge of seven-year-old Gideon and three-year-old David. As the years passed, Noah had supervised home-work and cleaned the house, including doing laundry. The only way he'd gotten out of cooking duty was to be really bad at it, on purpose.

"I assume they didn't tell you without prompting?" he asked, heading to the dining room to eat.

She followed. "Not exactly." She made a move to grab the pot of stew. "I can heat this for you."

"It's fine." He served himself the remainder of the salad, rolls and stew, then glanced up as she hovered. "Not exactly?" he repeated.

"One of the things we did today was discuss their schedules, not just their academics but extracurricular activities. In the grand scheme of things, we talked about responsibility. I sort of tossed out the idea that they could make their own beds and do their own dishes rather than letting them sit in the sink all night."

He gestured she should sit. "And they jumped at the chance to assume that responsibility?"

She hesitated. "Not all of them."

"Let me guess. Ashley and Zach were gung ho. Zoe got huffy. And Adam…"

"Said they'd be putting Cora out of work, and how could we live with that?"

Noah laughed, which made Tricia laugh, too. "That's my boy."

"Is he the most like you, out of all of them?"

The stew was lukewarm but tasty, the salad lukewarm and wilted, and the rolls cold but still crunchy. "I think Zach's the most like me. How'd your day go?"

"Great," she said. "They're certainly all individual, and yet the twin thing is strongly at work."

"They used to have secret languages when they were very young, but not anymore."

"Maybe not spoken, but they know how the other feels. I've never had a sibling, so I have nothing to compare it to."

"And I only know my brothers and I didn't have it. So, everyone got all their work done?"

"Yes. If you'd like to see it, I can bring it to your office later. Or I can meet you in the classroom."

"I'd like a summary, but I don't need to see the actual work. If you can come to my office right after the children go to bed, that would be great. I won't take up much of your time."

"All right." She stood. "For now I'd like to go to my room. I've been on duty for almost twelve hours."

He hadn't considered how long she worked. No wonder he lost nannies all the time. But Cora was supposed to keep an eye on the kids during lunch, giving the nan—teacher a break before afternoon activities. "Cora didn't relieve you for a while?" he asked.

"She offered, but I didn't want to interrupt the flow of the day. I'll let her from now on. I hadn't realized how tired I would be without a break."

"Good."

With a quick goodbye, she left. She hadn't looked tired. Her blond hair still held its curl, her eyes were as clear as ever. She wasn't slouching. In fact, her posture was perfect, her shoulders back, her breasts a tempting sight he tried to ignore, which was hard to do since her form-fitting T-shirt showed off every curve.

Noah usually ate dinner alone, which was fine with him. Tonight it bothered him. Maybe because he was sitting at the dining room table instead of standing at the kitchen counter. He finished up in a hurry, then debated what to do about the dishes. There were no leftovers. He should've left some stew so he could just put some foil on top and stick it in the refrigerator.

In the end, he put his dishes in the dishwasher but left the pot soaking in the sink.

He wandered into the family room. Zoe was playing a soccer video game on the small television. Adam was intent on his handheld Game Boy. Zach and Ashley were watching some-

thing on the Disney Channel, a movie about teenagers and basketball, with a lot of singing and dancing involved.

Noah sat on the couch next to Ashley, who moved a few
inches away, her lips pinched. He didn't know what to do with
her. It seemed like everything he did these days was wrong, and
she was so quick to judge him. And vocal. That was new.
Before, he could guess by her expression when she was upset
with him. Now she told him, as well. He should be grateful not
to have to guess anymore, but it left him confused, too.

"When this is over, would you come to my office, please?"
he asked her.

She waited a few seconds, then nodded.

He wanted to escape, but he made himself sit there, trying
to be part of their world. He didn't have a clue how they usually
spent their evenings after dinner. Like this? Watching TV,
playing games?

What did they used to do, as a family?

Well, really, did the past have any bearing on now? They
were older. Life had changed.

"Where's Miss Tricia?" Zach asked during a commercial.

"In her room," Noah answered.

"Why?"

"I guess she had things to do."

Zach eyed Noah like he was responsible, like he'd ordered
her to her room, or something.

"Oh," Zach said glumly. "Will she come down later?"

"I don't know. She's off duty as soon as I get home."

All four of the children turned and looked at him for a few
long seconds before they went back to watching television and
playing video games without uttering their opinion.

"Would you like to play a game?" he asked the room at large.
He knew the cabinet held tons of board games.

"Why?" Adam asked, not looking away from his Game Boy.

"To spend some time together as a family. Having fun." He tried not to sound defensive.

"It's too close to bedtime," Ashley said. "We probably couldn't finish."

No one else commented. No one made a move to play a game. So he sat and watched the rest of the movie with Ashley and Zach, trying to seem interested.

"I'm ready now, Father," Ashley said, getting up and heading out.

"What's she ready for?" Adam asked.

"I want to talk to each of you individually," Noah answered, including all of them in the answer. "It's nothing bad. I just want to know about your day and what you learned."

"Like you used to," Zoe said, not taking her eyes off her video match.

"Yes." So they remembered. Guilt came to sit on his shoulder.

"Are you going to test us?" Adam asked.

Noah almost sighed. "No. Just talk."

"For how long?"

"For as long as it takes. Ashley's coming first."

"Ashley always goes first," Zach muttered.

What happened to his agreeable, obedient children? When had he lost control? Or maybe it wasn't a matter of control but that they felt he'd abandoned them.

And wasn't it interesting to note that their newly found outspokenness had coincided with Tricia's arrival?

"Tomorrow you can go first," Noah said to Zach.

Ashley was already seated in a chair opposite his desk, waiting. As he sat, he glanced at a photograph of Margie on his desktop. His daughters looked so much like her.

"Have I done something wrong?" Ashley asked.

He shook his head. "I just wanted a report on your first day with Miss Tricia."

"It was fine."

"Is she a good teacher?"

"Yes."

He didn't know whether to laugh or sigh at her succinct responses. "Would you elaborate a little?"

"She told us she would demand a lot of us because we're all very smart."

He liked that. "That's it?"

"Well, she said the room was too…orderly, I think. That we could start leaving our art and science projects out instead of putting them away each night."

Since that was a rule Noah had created, he wasn't happy about it. Children needed order, not chaos, to learn. "Anything else? I'm interested in your impression of how she teaches and how she relates to you."

"She's…I like her. I don't know what else to say about her. She's my favorite teacher, so far."

"She's been here for a day and she's your favorite?" What did that say about the seven who preceded her?

"You can tell she really likes us. She doesn't pretend."

Was that why the other teachers had left? Not because of him, after all, but because they hadn't liked his children? "You have good judgment about such things. Thank you for telling me."

She beamed. It had been a while since she'd smiled like that at him.

"Zach wants to be next," he said. "I'll be up to say goodnight later."

"Okay, Father."

She left the room, her footsteps not even registering. In the silence, her words seemed to echo—*Father.* It did sound formal. *Had* he done what Tricia had suggested? Made them call him Father instead of Dad because of his own painful reminders?

Zach appeared in the doorway looking like a child sent to the principal's office. He didn't take a step inside.

"Come in, son."

"Miss Tricia doesn't sit behind her desk. She says it's like a wall between us."

Noah was already tired of hearing how perfect Miss Tricia was. "Where would you like me to sit, Zach?"

"On the couch."

"Will you sit there, too?"

He nodded.

Noah walked around his desk and took a seat at one end of the couch. Zach sat, as well, then smiled shyly.

"How was your day?" Noah asked.

"Good."

"Anything in particular you enjoyed?"

"Miss Tricia showed me a new game on the computer where I can practice math during my free time."

They all had good computer skills for their ages, but Zach was by far the most advanced and ambitious. "Do you have any complaints?"

He thought about it for a minute then said, "No," decisively, his expression open.

"Any comments to add, Zach?"

"No, I'm good."

"Okay. Send either Zoe or Adam in, will you please? I'll be up to say good-night later."

He hurried off. After a minute Zoe popped in. He was still sitting on the couch and gestured to her that she should sit there, too. She eyed the chair in front of the desk for a moment, sighed, then plopped onto the sofa but didn't look at him. She was the most openly hostile to him, rarely hiding her feelings about anything. He counted on her to keep him aware of any unhappiness among them.

"How was your day?" he asked.

"It was okay."

"Did you like Miss Tricia as your teacher?"

"She's fine. So far."

He rested his arms on his thighs and leaned toward her a little, trying to get her to look at him. "Do you expect she'll change?"

She shrugged. "Most of them do."

That surprised him. "Why didn't you tell me about that?"

"Guess it didn't matter so much." She kicked her feet, still not looking at him. "They're supposed to give us our lessons, then we do them. That's it. Doesn't make much difference who's in charge, does it?"

He thought it made a huge difference, but it was a topic for another time, when life had settled down again for all of them. "If you think Miss Tricia changes, Zoe, if she isn't being a good teacher, or a good person, I want you to tell me, okay?"

"Sure. Can I go now?"

He needed to make eye contact with her. It occurred to him how little she looked at him. Why hadn't he seen that before? "Look at me, please."

After a minute she did.

"Promise you'll tell me, Zoe."

"I said I would. *Now* can I go?"

He wanted to hug her. He knew she would resist, because at some point he'd stopped hugging them. He didn't even know why.

"Send Adam in, please."

She dashed out. Adam came through the door immediately, making an imaginary jump shot as he entered, then he vaulted over the sofa arm and landed in the seat with a whoosh.

"You got here fast," Noah commented.

"I was outside listen—I mean, waiting my turn." He grinned, obviously not contrite.

Noah decided not to have the it's-rude-to-eavesdrop talk

with his son tonight. Zoe would've seen him right outside the door. If she'd cared, she would've said something.

"So, I guess you want to know what I think of Miss Tricia," Adam said. Like Zoe, he fidgeted. "She's cool. She said she'd get me signed up for basketball next week. And she promised to bring her guitar next time she goes home. She said it wasn't practical to ask for a guitar and lessons until I saw I was really interested. She's gonna give me a few lessons first."

Was there anything Miss Tricia couldn't do? Noah wondered. "I didn't know you wanted to play guitar. I thought you liked the clarinet."

"Come on, Father. That's so last year."

Father. There it was again. It sounded especially formal they way he'd used it.

"Can I go now?" Adam asked.

Noah made a goodbye gesture, trying not to sigh. He shouldn't expect miracles with his children. Obviously he'd ignored them for too long—plus they'd done some growing up. He had to make some adjustments.

He returned to his desk, pulled a folder from his briefcase and wondered if Tricia hadn't come along when she had if he ever would've seen the light.

She had come along, however, and if he smiled and was nice to her, according to his children, he wouldn't ever have to look for another teacher.

That was a goal worth making changes for.

Chapter Six

Tricia sat in the chair opposite Noah's desk, waiting for him, her notepad listing all her questions on her lap. She'd said her good-nights to the children, bumping into Noah as she left the girls' room and he was going in. She was glad he was tucking them in. They needed him to be more involved. Plus he would reap benefits himself from a closer relationship.

Noah breezed into the office. He stopped, hesitated, then sat behind his desk.

"You've made a big impression on my children already," he said.

"They're terrific kids."

"They've been through hell."

She nodded, understanding. "You said Zach was most like you. Is one of the girls like Margie?"

"Ashley."

"In what way?"

He leaned back. "Attention to detail. Not wanting to make waves. Needing peace between everyone. And yet she was also sure of herself and stubborn."

"What kinds of vacations did you take?"

"Vacations? As a family?" He frowned thoughtfully. "We did Disneyland and Disney World."

"Camping?"

"Margie wanted to. I didn't. We stayed home a lot. Probably because I was gone half the month to Europe—most months, anyway. I just wanted to hang out here."

Tricia wondered if Margie was okay with that or if she'd just never protested it, figuring there would be plenty of trips as the kids got older.

"She and the children would go to her parents' house in San Luis Obispo several times a year," he said. "The kids still do. In fact, they'll be gone Thanksgiving week." He gestured toward her notepad. "You have questions?"

"Did I pass first-day muster with them?"

"Is that a question on your list?"

She smiled at his teasing, almost not seeing the twinkle in his eyes. So, he did have a sense of humor. She'd been wondering.

"It's the first question," she said, flashing the pad toward him too fast for him to read.

"You got major thumbs-up," he said. "Major. Adam even proclaimed you to be 'cool.'"

"Awesome." She was more than pleased. After a minute she tapped a finger on the first real question she'd written. "Halloween."

"Friday, October thirty-first. I'm a little sketchy on the details, but I think it's been a tradition in this country since early in the last century."

She liked this playful side of him. "I'm trying to picture you trick-or-treating. I'll bet you were a pirate."

His good mood disappeared. "Nope. Never did trick-or-treat. We didn't live in a neighborhood, but out in the country, like this."

"Do your kids dress up in costume? Do I need to take care of that?"

He shuffled through some papers on his desktop. "Here." He passed her an invitation with a ghost flying across the cover for a party on Friday night.

"Did you RSVP?" she asked, noticing it had come from their education specialist, Cynthia Madras.

"I forgot."

And of course the requested RSVP date had come and gone. "Do the children want to go?"

"I haven't asked them."

Implied in his tone of voice was that it wasn't his job. Apparently the previous teachers had taken care of those kinds of matters. "I'll ask them in the morning," she said. "Cynthia is coming tomorrow anyway, so I'll talk to her, make sure it's not too late to RSVP. If you're okay with them going to the party?"

"Sure. She puts on a Halloween party every year for the students she oversees. She does a haunted house. Next year Ashley and Zoe will be thirteen, and Cynthia lets the teens become ghouls for the party."

"She sounds like a lot of fun. I'm looking forward to meeting her." She glanced at her list again. "Zoe says she has a soccer match on Saturday at noon. Do you and the family go to those?"

"Not usually. Someone picks her up and brings her home."

She could tell by his body language that she shouldn't take the discussion any further, but she only had three months to help this family. She had to speak up. "Zoe needs you to pay attention to her, Noah. All of you should be supporting each other in your endeavors. It's good for the other kids to be there to cheer her on, too. Same for Adam when basketball starts."

"Yes, teacher."

That annoyed her. "Sarcasm? Really? Your family is fractured, Noah. I'm trying to help."

He stiffened. "I don't think we're fractured. They're good kids. Everything's been fine."

Until you came along. The unspoken words reminded Tricia of her place. She could effect change in this family, good change, but she needed to do so without upsetting Noah. She just had to be patient, make a difference gradually. Then they would all adapt together. She had so little time to help them find each other again.

She also felt a strong need to help him lighten up. Everything didn't have to be so serious. She'd learned that the hard way, herself.

"Okay, maybe everything hasn't been exactly fine," he said after she'd been silent for too long. "But I'm working on it."

Tricia turned her notepad over. She wouldn't broach the other topics yet, especially since he was in denial about other issues anyway. One day at a time. One change at a time. "That's all I have for now." She waited to be dismissed.

"I have a question for you," he said. "Ashley told me you want them to leave their projects out instead of putting them away. Before you make big changes like that, you need to talk to me. In this particular instance, it's my belief that they need a clean and orderly place to study. Tomorrow you'll go back to having them put their things away at the end of the school day."

He was telling her how to run her class? She counted to five, silently. "Would you come up to the classroom with me, please?" she asked, standing, not really giving him a choice but making it seem like it.

He followed her. Once again she felt his gaze on her rear as she climbed the stairs. Just the idea of it aroused her—which she resented as much as appreciated. He was the wrong man at the wrong time. When she settled into her new job and her new life, she would be thrilled to have such attention from a man. But not now.

She stopped halfway up the staircase and turned around. He ended up eye level with her chest. His gaze rose slowly until it connected with hers.

"Did you forget something?" he asked.

My common sense. But she didn't say it out loud. After a few seconds, he smiled slightly, knowingly, and moved around her, continuing up the stairs, passing her by, even though he could have walked beside her, the staircase being wide enough for two. She had no choice but to follow.

It was a nice view. A very nice view. She wondered if he worked out. Since he seemed to have so little free time, she didn't see how he could fit it into his schedule. Maybe at lunchtime? He looked like he exercised. His rear was firm and molded. Her hands would curve perfectly over them....

Noah looked over his shoulder as he reached the first landing. "Are we even now?" he said, when what he wanted to say was, "Look, I'm not serious every second of the day."

She dared to look confused.

He refused to smile at her innocent expression, knowing she was toying with him. Women had flirted with him a lot in the past three years, since he'd been widowed. Tricia didn't seem to be flirting, but instead teasing. He'd never crossed any barriers with any teacher in the past, never even joked. Was teasing the way to hold on to her? Smiling and being nice, as the children said? Keeping things businesslike certainly hadn't amounted to success.

The problem was—what was teasing and what was flirting? That not-crystal-clear issue of sexual harassment always lurked in a business relationship between opposite genders.

She came up beside him on the landing then. "Even?" she repeated. "I don't know. Are we?"

"I'm even," he said. "You, on the other hand, may be a little odd."

She grinned, which relaxed him. So the kids were right? Smile. Be more approachable. Less of a...boss, the easier role for him.

They walked side by side until they reached the single-wide staircase to the schoolroom. They stopped at the same time and looked at each other.

Noah reached into his pocket and pulled out a quarter. "Call it," he said.

"Heads, I...you go first."

He didn't miss her carefully worded pronouncement.

Noah flipped the coin, caught it then slapped it on the back on his hand. Tails. He won. He followed her up the stairs as she exaggerated the sway of her hips, making a game of it, as if to make him laugh. He didn't, nor was it a game to him. He wanted to put her hands on her, feel the movement, pull himself up close and wrap her in his arms....

Arousal hit him, hard and fast, a situation he had no way of hiding before they reached the classroom. He'd already flipped the light switch at the bottom of the stairs. No chance to stall, not even for a second.

She reached the top first and turned around, smiling, then her expression froze. He had no idea what to say, if he should even say anything at all. She was apparently having the same dilemma—in both respects. She wasn't saying anything, and her nipples had hardened, drawing his attention.

They stared at each other for long seconds, then he continued up the stairs until he stood in front of her. It was all he could do to keep from touching her. She had incredible breasts, high and firm, and she didn't wear loose clothing, but tops that molded, although not low cut at all.

Damn.

By unspoken agreement, they ignored the moment of attraction and moved into the classroom.

Neatness reigned on one end of the room, chaos on the other.

"This is exactly what I mean," he said. "No one can learn in this environment."

"You mean *you* couldn't learn in this environment."

He crossed his arms.

"See the first table on the left, Noah? That's Adam's."

The table was littered with Legos, none in containers but scattered, some kind of structure rising from the pile.

"Are you sure? It looks like Zach's handiwork."

She smiled. "They're supposed to do something outside their comfort zone. Adam is having to sit still and create something, which is what Zach likes to do."

"What's he building, do you know?"

"I'm not sure *he* does, yet. Maybe tomorrow it will take form enough for him to see." They moved to the next table, on which was a small stack of paper printed from the computer. "Zach is designing a putting green that they'll all work on starting tomorrow. Group project."

"Zach likes to work alone."

"Exactly."

"That one must be Zoe's," he said pointing to a small construction zone.

"Ashley's. She's using slats, nails and a hammer to build a crate bed for her stuffed dog, Harry. By process of elimination, you can see that Zoe is painting."

"Modern art, obviously," he said, eyeing the painting on the easel.

Tricia laughed. "Doesn't matter. She's doing it, even though Ashley's driving her crazy, giving advice. And Zach's happy because he gets to research putting greens on the computer, but his discomfort will come when we start the actual work and he has to be outdoors, digging in dirt."

"Not his favorite thing to do."

"Right. But my point is, you can see how long they would stall each day before tackling the work if they have to get it out and set it up every day."

"They would take their time. Run out the clock." Had they learned the art of the stall from him, the way he stalled about coming home?

"Probably so. This way there's no downtime. They come back from lunch and work on their projects for a half hour, and then we head outside to do something physical or whatever's on the agenda. I look at this part of the room and I don't see a mess. I see busy minds creating, testing themselves. What's wrong with that?"

He would sound ridiculous arguing her point, which was valid. "I'll give you that. As long as the rest of the workspace remains organized."

"Ahh. A compromise." She stuck out her hand. "Deal."

He shook her hand. She pulled free first, tucked both her hands in her pockets.

"Where are you thinking about building the putting green?" he asked.

"To the right of your deck, if that's okay."

"The lawn's dead."

"I thought we could pick up some sod."

"You think it's as easy as that?" He tried to remember when they'd moved into the house five years ago what Margie had done with the garden. He hadn't really paid attention. "I have a friend who's a landscaper, Joseph McCoy. Let me call him in the morning and have him stop by tomorrow, if he can. It can still be a learning experience, but you might as well put in a lawn that's going to live."

"That would be great, thanks. As long as he knows the kids are all going to be involved in it."

"I'll let him know. Maybe you could talk to him about doing a whole new garden. It's looking bad these days."

"Sure. I'll ask him to draw up some plans. Although I have to warn you, I know little about gardening."

They'd run out of topics. He stalled, not wanting to go work in his office, as he needed to. "So, you said Cynthia will be here tomorrow?"

"All morning, apparently. She's required to spend an hour per child each month. I'm glad she's coming when everything is new for me. I can make adjustments before something becomes routine." She covered her mouth as she yawned. "I'm sorry. I need to go to bed. I've been out of teaching for a while. It'll take a little getting used to."

"You know, I never saw a resume on you. Maybe tomorrow after dinner we could talk about your background."

"That's a plan. I'll see you tomorrow, then." She started to walk away, then turned back. "You'll make an effort to be here for dinner? Or call?"

After the cool greeting he'd gotten tonight? Did he have a choice? "Yes, on both counts."

"Great. Good night."

He watched her until she disappeared down the staircase, then he took a closer look at each child's project. He liked that Tricia was making them do something out of their comfort zones. She was innovative, unlike most of the other teachers, who had a plan and followed it. "Teaching to standards," it was called, which they all had done, but not much beyond. Most homeschoolers were taught by their own parents, who'd made that choice for a reason, and put a lot of effort into the job.

Hiring a teacher was different. It became a job then, although Tricia wasn't making it seem like that.

Early in the game, though, Noah reminded himself.

He picked up Ashley's crate-in-progress. Her slats were nailed at precise intervals, as he would have expected. So...out of her comfort zone but still with the exactness she always demanded of herself.

Ashley had changed the most recently. Well, Zach, too, a little. His was probably infatuation for the teacher, but Ashley was asserting herself as a leader more than ever. Maybe she'd completed the grief process. It was hard to tell with any of them, because they really didn't talk about their mother much at all. Even when he mentioned her, they didn't carry the conversation forward.

Noah opened the top drawer of each child's desk and pulled out folders, reviewing their weekly assignments. Adam really needed to work on his penmanship. The others were legible. A portable filing system sat on Tricia's desk. He was entitled to look through it but decided against it. Too soon. He would talk to Cynthia after her visit and get her opinion, but he had a feeling his search was over. He'd found the right person.

Now he just had the simple task of keeping her happy.

Chapter Seven

The next day, the children were crammed around the computer looking at Halloween costume possibilities as Tricia and Cynthia talked. Tricia tried to guess how old the petite, athletic-looking, redheaded Cynthia was. Thirty, maybe? They'd discussed the academics and requirements, but Cynthia hadn't made a move to leave yet. And although she'd been warm with the children, she'd been cool with Tricia.

"If Jessica had told me she was leaving," Cynthia said, "I would've gotten myself involved in the search for a replacement. They've had too many teachers, too much disruption. I hope you intend to stay for a long time."

Guilt hammered Tricia. Should she tell Cynthia about how she was staying only until January? Tricia didn't want the kids to overhear news that should come from their father, but maybe Cynthia *could* help find a permanent replacement.

Or Tricia could talk to Noah about it, suggest the best way to find someone permanent, someone right for all—

"You wore that last Halloween," Zoe said to one of her siblings, exasperation in her raised voice. "*And* the year before."

"So?" Adam replied, belligerent.

"So, think outside the box," Zoe countered.

"What does that mean, stupidhead?"

Cynthia leaned toward Tricia. "Adam has dressed up as a basketball player, two years running,"

"Gee, what a surprise," Tricia said, tongue in cheek.

"Will you be coming to the haunted house?" Cynthia asked.

"No." Tricia was going to force Noah to interact with his children by staying at his house and keeping to her off-duty schedule, especially since she wasn't going to go to Sacramento until after the bachelorette party Saturday night. "Noah will bring them."

"Well, there's a first."

Tricia couldn't decide if Cynthia was surprised or being sarcastic. "Sarcastic" didn't jibe with what Tricia had been told about the woman. Noah and Jessica had sung her praises, and the children were comfortable with her.

So, it must be something personal. Maybe Cynthia didn't like clutter, either.

The thought made her smile.

"I should get going," Cynthia said, gathering her briefcase. She had looked at all the work from the past month, regraded homework and tests, and taken samples for a portfolio she put together yearly on each child. "I'll take care of your purchase orders and drop by your supplies when they arrive, so I'll probably see you next week with those. I tend to make deliveries once a week. Bye."

She walked over to say goodbye to the children. Ashley hugged her. The others barely acknowledged her, including

Zach, but they were intent on their task to come up with costume possibilities. Tricia was secretively happy that Zach didn't hug her, which was really small of her. But there was something about Cynthia that bothered Tricia, like she'd have to watch her back.

Most people took to her. Kids liked her. Dogs adored her. Salespeople remembered her. She didn't think she'd done anything to offend Cynthia Madras, but…

Adam marched over to Tricia's desk and plopped there on his elbows. "If I want to be a basketball player, I can be one, right?" he asked, challenging her.

"Yes."

"See?" he shouted at Zoe, who rolled her eyes.

"I don't want to hear any more name-calling, Adam," Tricia said quietly.

"I didn't—"

"Yes, you did."

He frowned. "You mean 'stupidhead'?"

She nodded.

"That's just my nickname for her. It means I like her."

It was all Tricia could do not to laugh at his innocent expression. "Well, come up with a nicer one."

He walked away, muttering, "Everyone's picking on me." He plunked himself down at his activity table and started fiddling with Lego pieces.

The intercom crackled. "Tricia?" came Cora's voice. "Joseph McCoy is here to talk about the yard. And your lunches are ready."

Tricia punched a button. "Thanks. Be right down." Then to the children, she said, "Zach, please bring your plans for the putting green. Then as soon as we've consulted with Mr. McCoy, we're going on a picnic."

"All right!" Adam said.

"Isn't it a little cold?" Ashley asked.

Zach frowned.

Zoe didn't react at all.

"The sun's out, Ashley. It's really nice. Everyone grab a backpack and a sweatshirt, then hurry downstairs," Tricia said, heading down, then hearing arguing as she got closer to the kitchen.

"You stay out of my kitchen, Joseph McCoy," Tricia heard Cora almost shout.

"What? It's just a little dirt, Cora. It'll clean right up."

"Yes, by *me*. You can wait outside."

"Is everything okay?" Tricia asked as she stepped into the kitchen. "Do I have to send you to your corners?"

Joseph raised a hand in greeting. "Hey. You must be Tricia. Noah sent me."

Late twenties, Tricia decided. He was about her height and built like a man who worked hard all day, sturdy and toned. He had a long brown ponytail and wore shorts, a T-shirt and mud-caked boots.

"You're prompt," she said. "The kids will be down in a minute. They need to be involved in this project."

"No problem."

"So, you know Joseph?" Tricia said to Cora, whom Tricia had guessed to be in her early fifties.

"It's a small town. And he's always been obnoxious." She wielded her mop at him, and he laughed.

The kids came scurrying down the stairs then, making a race of it, jostling each other as they rushed through the dining room, coming to an abrupt halt when she gave them a look meant to stop them.

"Hey, kids!" Joseph shouted. "Let's go. Time's a wastin'."

They all sneaked past her, only Zach giving her a little smile.

"Thanks for packing the lunches," Tricia said as she passed by Cora.

"Happy to."

Tricia went outdoors and into the backyard. The kids were hanging around Joseph, barely giving him room to walk—except for Zach, who followed more slowly, his design clutched in his hands. Was he nervous? Unsure?

Joseph climbed the steps to the deck and looked out at the property. "Be quiet a minute," he said to the noisy children. "Let me think."

Tricia could hear the silence, that is, the slight breeze in the air, some rustling of leaves—from the breeze or an animal? She scoped the terrain, wondering. She would rather be hearing car horns and sirens, which would block sounds she wasn't comfortable with. Ignorance is bliss.

"All right. Zachary, let me see your design, please." Joseph held out a hand.

Zach dropped it in Joseph's hands like a surgical nurse handing over a scalpel, then he stepped back and looked away.

Unsure, Tricia decided. Testing new waters.

"I didn't know you were a golfer, Zach," Joseph said while studying the design.

"I'm not."

"No? You want this built for Adam, then, I guess?"

"No. I just thought it would be something fun to do. As a family."

Surprisingly, all the children stayed silent, but they looked at each other in a moment that was so telling to Tricia, it almost broke her heart. They desperately wanted their father involved in their lives.

"Does your father play golf?" Tricia asked Zach.

"He used to."

Tricia traded looks with Joseph, who seemed to have gotten a clear picture himself. "Okay, crew, let's go scout out the turf.

Zachary, my man, you did an amazing job of research and design. Let's go see how we can make it come to life."

Tricia hung back, letting Joseph be the boss. Instead of going on a picnic, they all ate their lunches on the deck, with Cora bringing one for Joseph, as well. He talked to them for a long time about the process of getting the space ready for sod, and why it was important. They calculated how much sod they would need, then they discussed a design for the rest of the yard, as Noah had requested.

Adam asked that Joseph include an estimate for a full basketball court, not just the backboard and hoop on the garage. Zoe wanted a pool included. Ashley wanted a rose garden. Zach made no request. The putting green seemed to be enough for him.

They were wrapping things up when the sound of a car turning into the driveway reached them. Noah. And it was only three o'clock. Zach headed toward the garage, at first walking, then picking up his pace. Ashley went next. Adam and Zoe not only stayed where they were but studiously avoided looking at him.

"Go greet your father," she said softly to them. They seemed relieved to be told to do so, as if they'd wanted to but didn't know how to change a habit.

Tricia caught Joseph studying the scene but also gathering his paperwork and rolling it into a tube. She moved to the deck railing and waited, enjoying hearing Zach so excited and talkative as he told Noah about the project. And Ashley was holding her father's hand, while Adam carried his briefcase. Zoe lingered at the fringes. Tricia would've said Ashley was trying the hardest to connect with Noah, if Zach hadn't made his need known himself.

Noah set a hand on Zach's head, quieting his steady stream of dialogue, as he described the plans in detail. "Am I early enough?" he asked Tricia as he approached.

He looked happy. The children mostly looked happy, maybe a little intense, too, but, for the most part, smiling.

She didn't want to crack a joke in front of them, so she just smiled and nodded.

"Joseph," Noah said, holding out a hand. "Thanks for coming so fast."

"It sounded important. If you've got time, I'd like your input before I run an estimate for you."

"Sure. Come in to my office."

Joseph winked at Tricia. "I just have to take my boots off first."

"Okay, kids," she said. "I need to take Zoe to soccer practice and Adam to karate. Zach and Ashley? You can stay here or tag along. Which do you want?"

"I want to stay," Zach said, eyeing his father. "Can I come to your meeting with Joseph?"

"For a little while, then Joseph and I will finish up alone."

"Okay."

"Ashley?" Tricia asked.

"I'll go with Adam."

"Really? Okay." Tricia glanced at Noah, surprised.

"Her *boyfriend*'s in my karate class," Adam said.

Ashley reacted like any sister. She denied, denied, denied until an argument ensued. Tricia waited for Noah to step in. When he didn't, she did, sending Adam off to change into his uniform, his *gi,* and Zoe to get into her own gear.

"Did you have a good day?" Noah asked her as Joseph sat to take off his boots.

"We did, thanks."

"You, Tricia. Did *you* have a good day?"

She didn't understand the difference, but answered yes, then added, "Cynthia was here."

"She called me."

There was something in his voice... Is that why he was home early? Because of something Cynthia told him? "Did she have a complaint?"

He hesitated. "We'll talk tonight, after the children go to bed."

Great. Now she had to spend the rest of the day worrying. Then she changed her thinking. She was a good teacher, and the children were responding well to her. She had nothing to be concerned about.

"Okay. Tonight, then," she said. "Excuse me."

Tricia moved away from him. She didn't like keeping things locked up inside, had given that up during the past year. But she couldn't get insistent with Noah now, not with Joseph's obvious curiosity about the family dynamics.

So, until tonight, long after dinner, even, she was stuck having to live with anticipation. It wasn't a good feeling.

Noah decided Zach was right. Sitting on the couch instead of behind his desk created a different environment. Each child had been more open during their how-I-spent-my-day conversation with him, even Zoe. So when Tricia came in his office after the kids had been tucked into bed, Noah indicated she should sit on the couch, then he sat at the other end.

"I take it Cynthia was critical," she said, her voice a little on edge, not even waiting for him to start the conversation.

"She said their class work was excellent."

Tricia's hands were folded primly in her lap. "Which I had nothing to do with, having been their teacher for only one day."

"Why do you assume she criticized you, Tricia?"

"She was very warm to the children, and they obviously like her. But she was very cool to me. I didn't say or do anything I thought would be considered rude or presumptuous."

Noah stretched his arm along the back of the sofa. If he moved over a few inches, he could touch her—and she seemed to need some kind of consoling. Touching her, however, broke all the rules.

"Cynthia expressed some concern," he said, "about the way you were structuring the class."

"What does that mean? I'm following the schedule that Jessica used. Academics in the morning. Then after lunch, hands-on work, physical activity, lessons, play dates with friends. I've got some field trips planned, too. It's no different at all, except a little more adventurous, maybe." She frowned then. "Or do you mean she agreed with you about the kids leaving their projects out? Did she think that made me look lazy? That I wasn't encouraging the children toward neatness?"

"I don't know for sure, although she does know what rules I have in place. We are going to meet later in the week to discuss it. For the record, Tricia, I'm happy with what you're doing, so far."

"How can you even judge that at this point?"

"The children judge it. I take my cues from them."

That made her relax into the cushions again, her hair bouncing with the movement. He wanted to wrap a long curl around his finger and pull her closer.

Instead he clenched his fist. "So, we were going to talk about your work experience tonight."

"David really did leave you in the dark, didn't he? Has your brother always been so pushy?"

"He's always been assertive, but not usually aggressive, except in business. As the oldest, I've always been the dominant one, especially since our father died."

"You haven't mentioned your mother."

"My mother lives in New York." He was aware of the harshness seeping into his own voice, but didn't try to soften it. "My parents were divorced when I was two, and my father got sole custody. He married again the next year, and they had Gideon a year later. That marriage lasted three years, and he got sole custody of Gid. Then my father married David's mother the same year—she was already pregnant. That marriage lasted a surprising eleven years—eleven years of screaming, yelling and throwing things at each other. They divorced the year I escaped to go to college. Again, he got sole custody."

Her eyes had gone wide. "Do you see your mother?"

"She came for Margie's funeral. I hadn't seen her for five years before that."

"She ignores her grandchildren, too?"

"Pretty much. I'm grateful to Margie's parents, who are very involved." He was done with the topic. "How about you?"

It took her a few seconds to catch up with the abrupt change of subject. "My father died when I was eleven, as I told you. My mother died almost a year ago. I had stopped teaching to take care of her after a severe stroke. She hung in there for four years. I have one grandfather living. He's a spry old guy. Lives in Arizona. Golfs almost every day. He married a woman twenty years younger. They seem very happy."

"How long did you teach kindergarten?"

"Six years. I'm thirty-four, in case you've been wondering, but I haven't taught in the classroom since my mother got sick five years ago."

"What'd you do the past year?"

"Healed."

He leaned forward, resting his arms on his thighs. "How?"

"I have to backtrack a little to answer that. While I was in college I met a man, Darrell, and fell in love. We got engaged. He went into the army while I was in the credential program. We planned our wedding for right after I finished school, then he was killed in a helicopter training accident before the wedding. I buried myself in my work, ignoring the grief, then my mom got sick. She outlived all predictions by at least three years."

Noah was grateful for the eleven years and four children

before he'd lost Margie, but he was sympathetic to Tricia's losses, too. "I'm sorry."

"Thank you. Anyway, you asked how I healed." Her expression opened. She smiled. "I saw America. I drove all over the country, stopping whenever something interested me, talking to people in all walks of life. I stayed overnight one place and two weeks at the next, depending on my whims. I learned to laugh again. I decided to shake up my life."

He wondered what that would be like—shaking up his life. He had too many commitments, too many people counting on him. He couldn't make much in the way of change. Not that he wanted to remove himself from the business or the children he loved, but having no options sometimes felt overwhelming. Sometimes he even missed all the European travel he used to do.

"Maybe you could try shaking up your life a little," she suggested.

"How?"

"Do something different. Start small, like going to Zoe's soccer game, then take the kids out for pizza. Whatever you've been doing, change it up."

"That sounds chaotic to me."

She smiled. "It will be. Until it's normal. Your new normal."

Normal. Well, what did he have to lose?

Chapter Eight

Chaos, Noah thought, listening to the children run around upstairs. Absolute chaos.

"You're really going to abandon me to this?" he asked Tricia, who sat in the living room casually flipping through a magazine like a woman who was off the clock. Which she was.

"They're just excited," Tricia said, humor lacing the words. "It's Halloween."

"How much candy have they already had?"

She laughed. "None."

"Are you sure I can't just drop them off at the party and go back and get them later?"

"You could, but they'd be very disappointed. You'll have a good time, Noah. There's something so fun about kids dressing up in costumes. Seems to take away their inhibitions."

"That's a good thing?"

She grinned.

Noah paced at the bottom of the stairs. The past few days had been great—except for his argument with Tricia about a hike she'd taken the kids on. He didn't feel she knew the area well enough to go off exploring. She'd said she had a great sense of direction. And they hadn't gotten lost, had they? Not for a second.

Still. What if something had happened to her? How would they have known how to get home?

"Cell phone and my portable GPS locator?" she'd replied, her eyebrows arching high. "Noah, they need to experiment and get experience. If there's no risk, there's no growth. I'm not talking about physical risks or danger, but testing limits and taking chances, things necessary to really living life, not just observing it. I was getting over my own fears, too, about whatever unseen creatures are around."

He'd spent a lot of time considering her words. He knew he was overly cautious. In theory he agreed with Tricia, but he had a hard time putting it into practice. He wanted his children safe.

Noah looked at his watch then hollered up the stairs, "Party started fifteen minutes ago." He eyed Tricia. "How are you going to spend your evening?"

"Watch a video. Eat popcorn. Take a bubble bath." She smiled serenely.

The image of her amid a mound of bubbles held fast in his mind. "You know we'll only be gone a couple of hours."

"Since the movie I want to watch isn't appropriate for the kids, I'll do that first, and take my bath after you get back, so I know someone else is around."

Great. He'd be at home when she was in the bathtub, naked and wet. "You're still afraid of being here alone?"

"One trip into the woods isn't going to change that. I hear every sound, especially at night."

"Does it keep you awake?"

"Sometimes."

If you come to bed with me, you'll sleep easier. He didn't say the words, of course, but the enticing thought added to his arousal, something that no longer surprised him.

The kids finally came flying down the stairs. As expected, Adam wore a Sacramento Kings jersey and carried a basketball. Zach wore a white lab coat and wire-rimmed glasses, and his hair was spiked with gel, giving him a mad-scientist look. Ashley had donned a delicate costume from last spring's ballet production, but had added wings. As for Zoe, she wore a bathing suit over tights and a long-sleeve T-shirt. She carried a mask, snorkel and flippers, with a handmade scuba tank on her back, its original shape probably an empty oatmeal container covered in foil. Yet another hint for a swimming pool.

He had a big surprise for her, come Christmas.

They made a half circle around him, apparently awaiting his approval.

"Don't you all look fabulous!" Tricia exclaimed, coming to stand beside him. "Zach, your hair is perfect. Nice touch."

"Zoe did it, since I helped her design her scuba tank."

"You mean you didn't help them make their costumes?" Noah asked Tricia.

"Miss Tricia had to approve our choice, but we had to make them," Ashley said. "I didn't make my tutu, but I added the angel wings. Zach designed them, and Adam helped put them together."

"You're all very clever," Noah said. "Where'd you get the lab coat, Zach?"

"From the costume trunk. Mom put a whole bunch of stuff in there, remember?"

Mom. Noah made a decision. "I've been thinking maybe you all should call me Dad instead of Father."

"How come?" Zoe asked.

He shrugged.

They all looked at each other for a few seconds.

"It's okay with me," Adam said.

"Me, too. Dad," Zach said with a quick grin.

Noah looked at Zoe. "Sure," she said. "If that's what you want. Gonna seem a little weird at first."

"I know. Just try it out. If you don't like it, you don't have to. Ashley?" He figured she would be his toughest sell, since she had the most problem with change.

"I'll think about it," she said.

"Can we go now?" Adam asked.

"Sure. Tell Miss Tricia goodbye."

"Have fun," she called out. "You, too," she added to Noah when the kids had raced toward the kitchen.

"No comment on the *Father/Dad* thing?"

"I think you made the right decision."

He appreciated that she didn't say I-told-you-so. "Sometimes you can be so diplomatic."

"Sometimes." She gestured toward the kitchen. "They're probably buckled in by now and starting to wonder where you are."

He gave her a long look. "Enjoy your evening."

"I intend to, thank you."

He didn't want to leave. Or rather, he wanted her to go with him. He hadn't had much experience being the parent who hauled the children, not alone, anyway. He realized what a disservice he'd done to them by not being involved. It had taken Tricia's honesty to give him a kick in the pants.

"Thank you," he said, remembering it was his job to be nice to her so that she would stay.

"You're welcome. For what?"

"I think you know. See you later."

She was right. They were all buckled in and raring to go. The drive to Cynthia's took less than twenty minutes. It was the perfect place for a haunted house—a two-story Victorian, probably built around the turn of the twentieth century and restored a couple of times through the years. It looked in need of some TLC now.

The kids ran ahead of him. Howls penetrated the night, and clashes of thunder and lightning.

"Hurry up, Dad," Zach called, having adapted immediately, apparently, to the change in title.

Noah liked the sound of it, like he was a more hip father or something. He picked up his pace and joined the kids at the front door, which was open. Spooky sounds came from within.

"You can stay here," Adam said, apparently deciding that having Dad by his side made him a sissy or something. "We've done this before, you know. We're not scared."

"Should I wait outside?"

"The parents wait in the living room. Over there."

A child shrieked then laughed nervously. Noah headed to the uncool lounge with the other parents. He didn't know any of them, and he silently cursed Tricia for leaving him to this torture on his own.

He nodded to a few people, grabbed a couple of jack-o'-lantern cookies and headed for the front door. He'd give the kids some time then return to the room, and grin and bear it. Small talk with strangers had never been his strong suit, unless they were ordering a Falcon car.

"Noah, hi!" Cynthia caught him just as he was about to step outside.

"Hey. The place looks great," he said. "Sufficiently scary."

"Thanks. I'm glad you came."

Like he had any choice. "Listen, I'm sorry I had to cancel our meeting yesterday. We had a long conference call with some people overseas. The time difference often ruins my best-laid plans."

"No problem. I really would like to meet with you soon,

however. As I said, I have some concerns. Maybe instead of me coming all the way to your office, we could just meet for dessert and coffee somewhere around here after dinner one night next week?"

Was she hitting on him? She'd moved in a little closer, but there was a lot of noise, too, making it hard to hear and be heard. "I could probably manage that," he said, almost stumbling as he backed up a little, bumping into the threshold.

She grabbed his arm. "Careful."

She didn't let go, so he knew without a doubt that she *was* hitting on him. "I'm fine, thanks."

He wondered what movie Tricia was watching. Something the kids couldn't watch, she'd said. Nudity? Love scenes? He'd learned to avoid those movies, didn't need to be reminded of what he was missing.

"What night are you free?" Cynthia asked.

She drew closer as someone wanted to get by them. Her breast pressed into his arm. The rest of her body, too, for a few seconds, then she stepped back, although not too far. She was a petite woman. Maybe five-three, maybe a hundred pounds. Still, she had curves in all the right places. Nothing like Tricia's, but—

"Noah?"

"I'm free every night, I think," he said, focusing on her again.

"How about Tuesday, then? Would you like to meet at the Lode?" which was the locals' term for the Take a Lode Off Diner, a play on words since Chance City was in the heart of California's Mother Lode region.

"Sure," he said. "How about eight o'clock?"

"Perfect. Tuesday at eight, then." She gave him a quick hug, startling him, then she disappeared into the manufactured-fog-filled room where his children had first gone.

What was going on? She'd always been so professional with him.

Maybe he was reading too much into it. He had sex on the brain now that Tricia had come into his life.

Noah returned to the parents' room in time to see Cynthia giving a big hug to a couple about to leave, and then their two children.

Okay, he thought. She's just a hugger. No problem. Except… she'd never hugged him before.

After a while his children came charging into the room, laughing. He stared at them, thinking how beautiful they all were. How perfect. And how empty his world would be when they left to pursue their own lives one day.

Zach came at him full force and wrapped his arms around Noah's waist. Noah hugged him back and smiled at the others. The moment didn't last, however, as Adam looked away quickly and Zoe soon after. They both went to the tables and picked up a juice box and cookies. Ashley didn't take her eyes off Noah until he let Zach go. She looked just like Margie then. Exactly like her.

An eerie feeling swept through him, especially when her smile widened, as if it were Margie standing there, giving her approval of what was happening between them as a family.

"Did you thank Miss Cynthia?" he asked the group at large.

They went together to thank her. She gave them all hugs, although Zach tucked his arms in close and moved back right away. She looked at Noah over the top of Zach's head.

"Thanks," Noah mouthed, then waved. He gathered his brood, and they walked to the car, talking excitedly, reliving some of the scariest moments. Apparently Adam had jumped the highest when a ghoul had leaped at him. Tough-guy Adam was going to have to live it down, which was not something siblings let slide too easily.

At home they found Tricia in the family room. She'd lit a fire, set two huge bowls full of popcorn on the coffee table, and two thermal carafes of hot cocoa. She'd rented *Bedknobs and Broomsticks*, a movie as old as she and Noah.

Noah sent the kids up to change into pajamas. He sat next to Tricia on the couch.

"Did you have a good time?" she asked.

How could he tell her he was pretty sure Cynthia has been flirting with him? "It was fine." He made a broad gesture. "This was nice of you."

"I had fun."

He slid his arm along the couch. His fingers grazed her sweater. She didn't react, so either she hadn't felt it or was ignoring it. "Why didn't you go home to Sacramento tonight, since we were going out, anyway?"

She looked surprised. "I promised the children I wouldn't leave until Saturday mornings, but I also decided it's kind of crazy for me to go home tomorrow for a few hours then drive back for the bachelorette party at night. I'll go either right after the party or very early on Sunday. I've got some old wallpaper to remove and some woodwork to prep so that my painter can come in during the week while I'm gone."

"How soon are you putting it on the market?"

"As soon as it's ready to show. It was hopelessly outdated. I've been working on it since I got back into town, but some things I'd rather pay to have done. I'd like to remodel the kitchen and bathroom, but I'm settling for some upgrades. I can't delay too long. The way real estate is going, I'll be lucky to sell it by January. Not the best time of year."

Adam bounced into the room, leaped over the arm of the recliner, landed, then grinned at them. The patter of other feet followed. In a minute the room looked like a small theater.

Tricia stood and said good-night.

All of the kids except Zoe protested, so Noah ended up not having to. Giving in to the pressure, Tricia took her seat again.

Zach sat on the floor between them, his shoulders resting against Tricia's left leg and Noah's right. Popcorn and mugs of hot chocolate were passed around, then Ashley climbed over Zach and snuggled between Noah and Tricia. They started the movie.

"This is baby stuff," Adam complained after watching a few minutes.

Ashley shushed him.

Adam entertained himself by tossing popcorn into the air and catching it in his mouth. Agreeing with Adam's assessment of the movie, Noah threw a fluffy kernel into the air himself and caught it, then winked at Adam, who grinned back. Ashley got prickly and vocal. Zach was engrossed in the movie, apparently hearing nothing going on around him. Zoe ignored them all—pointedly.

The popcorn competition continued. Ashley put her arm through Tricia's and leaned her head against her shoulder. Noah caught Zoe glancing their way now and then.

He considered how life had changed in the Falcon household. The children had blossomed in such a short period of time. Ashley becoming outspoken, instead of always trying to please. Zach opening up, speaking for himself, finally. And hugging. As for Adam, he'd always been a busy kid, the least complicated, but now he was more vocal, too. Zoe was the toughest to identify change in. She was the only one who seemed to have taken a step backward—but maybe that would lead to changes in other ways.

Tricia McBride was one magical woman.

After the movie ended, Noah waited at the top of the stairs until Tricia had said her good-nights to the kids, then he stopped her on her way to her bedroom.

"Thank you for setting up the movie night," he said. "They— we all enjoyed it."

"Who won the popcorn contest?"

He smiled. "Adam. Or at least he had fewer pieces on the floor than I did. You know, for all that he said it was a movie for babies, he seemed to get pretty interested along the way."

"I was glad to see it. He gets bored so fast."

"All his life." Noah didn't know what else to say, but he didn't want to stop talking. He'd thought it would be hard to do what his children had asked of him, being nice to the teacher so she would want to stay. He was finding it way too easy.

She yawned. "Sorry. I'll say good-night now."

"You still going to take a bubble bath?" Why the hell had he asked that? It was none of his busi—

"That's my plan. Hope I don't doze off in the tub."

She gave him a sleepy smile that seemed incredibly sexy to him. He wanted to drag her into his arms and kiss her, pull her body against his so that they touched all the way down.

Her eyes went serious. She lifted a hand, almost touched his chest. "Noah—"

"Dad!"

Noah closed his eyes for a moment then turned his head toward his son's bedroom. "Coming, Zach."

When he looked back, he spotted Tricia hurrying to her bedroom. Now he'd never know what she would've said next. He would go to bed picturing her in a hot bubble bath, remember the anticipation of her hand almost touching him, and not wonder for a minute why he didn't get to sleep for hours.

Chapter Nine

Saturday night—date night—and the dateless Noah leaned his elbows on the bar behind him and surveyed the scene before him. Being the designated driver at a bachelor party stunk. He'd had one beer hours ago at Gideon's house, where they'd barbecued steaks and played poker until all four of the other bachelor-party-goers declared the evening the dullest in history.

"Where's the stripper?" David had asked, not meaning it, but definitely meaning the party needed to pick up some steam. So he announced that they were moving it to the Stompin' Grounds, a local watering hole. Noah hadn't been there in years.

It hadn't changed a bit. The walls were dark and paneled. The tables had history carved into their tops, initials and dates, hearts and Xs through them, added later. The jukebox still played tunes about good dogs, great trucks and cheating women.

Noah scanned the room. David and Gideon were being

competitive and noisy over a game of pool. Joseph and his brother Jake stood nearby, waiting to take their place.

Noah hadn't seen Tricia before he left—she'd still been getting ready—so he didn't know where the bachelorettes were going to party. It had been the subject of speculation all evening, the possibilities becoming increasingly creative, with Joseph saying he hoped they were having private lessons in the art of stripping. The image of Tricia peeling off her clothes had stuck in Noah's head and refused to budge.

A woman he didn't recognize headed his way then. She had to be old enough to drink legally, but she didn't look it. Her hair was black, her eyes bright blue. Her body was compact, one that would've appealed to him if Tricia hadn't come into his life.

"Hi, there. I'm Melanie." She rattled the ice in her empty glass. "Buy a thirsty girl a refill?"

"Sure." He figured if she was brave enough to ask, he could at least treat her. He signaled the bartender.

"How come you're all by your lonesome?" she asked.

"I'm not. My friends are over there. Bachelor party."

She checked them out. "Which one's the groom?"

"The one lining up the shot."

"Cute butt," Melanie said.

Noah grinned.

"Yours, too," she said. "Makes me want to grab ahold. What's your name?"

"Noah."

"Yeah? Biblical cool. Do you have pairs of everything?"

"Sort of. Two sets of twins, nine and twelve."

Her mouth dropped open. She pointedly looked at his left hand, which bore no ring. "Seriously? Wow. You really look good for your age."

"How old do you think I am?" he asked.

The bartender set her drink on the counter. She scooped it

up and took a sip, giving Noah a long, measuring look. "I'm thinking forty. Like my dad."

Ouch. Double insult. Four years older than his actual age.

"Not quite," he said, not knowing whether to laugh or start asking around about Botox. He caught Gideon looking his way. Gid could read him—or anyone—like a neon sign. He'd won the most at poker tonight, too, able to pick up on tells that no one else would notice.

Noah gestured toward him with his glass. "See the tall guy in the dark blue shirt, Melanie?"

"Uh-huh."

"He's not old enough to be your father. Tell him I sent you." Noah sat on a stool to watch the fun. Gid spotted her heading toward him, gave Noah an I'll-get-you-for-this look, then made his shot while Melanie hovered, talking to him the whole time.

Noah laughed. Then Gideon said something to the girl that made her face turn bright red, and off she went, back to a table with her girlfriends, where she leaned close and said something that made the others cover their mouths with their hands and look at Gid.

Noah wandered over to his brother. "What'd you say to her?"

"I asked if she'd like to try out my new whip. Brand-new. Never before used."

"You took a chance there. What if she was into that stuff?" Gid gave him a cool look.

"Oh, yeah," Noah said. "Sometimes I forget you can read people's minds."

The front door opened. Raucous laughter spilled into the already noisy bar, followed by five bachelorettes who appeared to be having a helluva lot more fun than the five bachelors.

Valerie came first, wearing a gaudy gem-encrusted tiara with a short, pink veil attached to the back. Noah had never seen her look so uninhibited or carefree. Laura Bannister, attorney, former Miss Universe contestant and former girlfriend of David, came through next—or rather, danced through, as if in a conga line.

Dixie, Joseph's on-again, off-again fiancée—burst in. Joe had proposed recently, and she'd accepted, then gave the ring back because he wouldn't set a date. They'd been together since they were fourteen—off and on.

Next came a very attractive brunette he'd never met, but since he knew the rest of the women, it had to be Denise Watson, the owner of At Your Service.

Then finally Tricia, who wore boots, jeans, a white blouse with blue pin stripes, and a tan suede jacket. She'd added long, silver earrings and a pendant that hung low enough to almost rest between her breasts. It was the first time she'd worn anything that showed cleavage.

The arrival of the women changed the tone of the evening. Valerie ran into David's arms and was kissed for so long that Noah had to turn away. He'd forgotten what that felt like, but the need for it hit him hard. Loneliness hit him even harder.

Dixie pointedly ignored Joseph, who eyed her with longing. No one had any doubt that they would reconcile, but Joe had to step up to the plate and name a wedding date. They were it for each other.

"Thanks for sending Tricia our way," Noah said to Denise.

"She sounds happy to be there, too. I'm glad it's working out."

Tricia came up beside him and smiled. A slightly woozy smile, like she'd had a drink—or two—too many. "You all having a good time?" she asked.

"Depends on who you talk to," Noah said. She smelled good, was wearing some kind of perfume, although mingled with the scent of champagne. "Your timing was perfect. How about you?"

"Oh, yeah." She laughed girlishly. "Good time. Definitely."

"Who drove?"

"Denise arranged for a limo. No need for a designated driver that way. Plus she'll be able to go home to Sacramento tonight. I would've liked to have hitched a ride with her so I could get busy on my house first thing tomorrow morning, but I wouldn't have my car to get back tomorrow night." She flattened a hand on his chest. "Did you know your children have never been inside a limo? Your company *makes* limos. What's with that?"

He was distracted by the touch of her hand, even through his shirt. "Let's dance," he said, moving her onto the tiny dance floor, not waiting for an answer.

She didn't protest, even though it was a slow dance. He figured he was taking advantage of her having a few drinks, which had undoubtedly clouded her ability to think too clearly. The dance floor filled quickly, forcing them closer together, although they weren't touching all the way down their bodies…. It had been a long time since he'd held a woman that close.

"What'd you do tonight?" he asked.

She smiled leisurely. "What happens at bachelorette parties stays at bachelorette parties."

"That good, huh?" Now she really had his curiosity up. "No hints at all?"

She got close and whispered dramatically, "I can only say it involved champagne and a pole."

A pole? Had they learned how to pole dance? He could picture Laura and Dixie doing that, but not Valerie—obviously he didn't know his future sister-in-law well. He didn't know anything about Denise except that she ran a successful business.

As for Tricia, he could picture her dancing seductively, enticingly, using the pole for all it was worth. Could picture it too well. But the only possibility he had of seeing it would be if she left his employ. It couldn't happen while she worked for him—and that was his goal, to get her to stay.

He couldn't win either way, but he could enjoy this moment, this night. He danced her around in a tight circle, showing off his moves. Dancing was something he did well. But the moment he started around a second time, she said, "Whoa, there, Fred Astaire. My stomach doesn't like that move."

"Serves you right." He slowed everything down to accommodate her, hoping the slightly green tinge on her face was from the strange lighting in the bar. "Okay?"

"Yeah. Thanks." Her smile was…adorable. He was sure he'd never used that word before.

David and Valerie bumped into them.

"Thanks for letting Hannah stay over tonight," David said to Noah. "I think I'll take my blushing, slightly drunk, almost-bride home and have some fun. You don't mind if we sleep in, do you? Pick her up later in the morning?"

Noah was envious as hell. He wanted to go home to his big bed and have someone in it with him. A certain someone who felt really good in his arms. "No, that's fine. I'll take you home."

"Denise offered the limo driver, since he's just hanging around waiting for us, anyway," Valerie said. The music stopped, so they all did, too. "You stay and have fun. I'm going to say my thanks and goodbyes." She hugged Tricia. "It was great getting to know you."

"I had a blast," Tricia said. "Thanks for including me." As soon as they left, Tricia turned to Noah. "How much longer do you plan to stay? I might as well go home with you. It'll save Fabian a stop."

"Fabian?"

"Our driver. Fabian Kowalski." She leaned close and whispered, "Our Pole."

Pole? Not a dance pole—a Pole. Noah started to laugh, then laughed so hard he began coughing. Tricia pounded him on the back. Gideon came over, concerned.

"I'm fine," Noah said, choking a little.

Denise joined them. "I'd like to get going. Tricia, are you ready or do you want to go home with Noah?"

"Actually," Noah answered before Tricia could. "Tricia, why don't you let Denise drop you off at your house in Sacramento? The kids and I will come pick you up tomorrow afternoon."

"Really? Are you sure that's not too much trouble?"

As much as Noah would've liked to have continued the evening with her, she'd been drinking, and his babysitter was spending the night. No privacy, which was probably a good thing. No moral dilemmas to contemplate.

"I'm going to take the kids on a field trip to my shop," he said, "and show them the cars in production, something I haven't done in years. We've got a limo ready for its owner. I think a test drive is in order."

Tricia beamed. "Good for you. Sounds like a great plan to me. I'll see you tomorrow, then."

Farewells were made, with Dixie still ignoring Joseph, then the women left. Joseph and Jake wanted to finish their match at the pool table, so Noah and Gideon wandered off a little to wait.

"Are you out of your mind?" Gideon asked the minute they sat at a table.

"Hey, I was just having a little fun with you. She may have been young, but she seemed—"

"Hell. I'm not talking about the girl you sicced on me. I'm talking about slow-dancing with your nanny. You, who gave David such grief about getting involved with his housekeeper. Are you crazy?"

Or something. "Teacher, not nanny. And we didn't get too close."

"She was toying with your collar and looking at you like you were her next meal."

"She was?"

Gideon dropped his head into his hands. "You can't be that dense. She's totally into you."

"I know there's a certain...*attraction* between us, but I haven't seen more than that."

"You're not looking."

"I noticed when Cynthia Madras was hitting on me last night."

"Yeah? Cynthia? She's very attractive."

"I hadn't really noticed until last night." But in comparison to Tricia?

"You should ask her out."

"Cynthia?"

"Are we talking about anyone else? It's time to date, Noah. And maybe it'll put the skids on your attraction to Tricia." Gideon's expression turned intense. "I can't believe you're willing to risk losing her. She seems perfect for the kids."

"No 'seems' about it. She *is* perfect."

"Then ask Cynthia out," Gid repeated, more emphatic this time.

"I'll think about it. We're meeting for coffee on Tuesday night to talk about the kids. But you know who would be better for me? Denise."

Gid's gaze sharpened. "Why?"

"She doesn't live here, for one thing. Makes it easier if things don't work out. Plus, she doesn't know the kids, so no potential problems there."

"She's not right for you."

It took a few seconds for his words to sink in. "How would you know that? Did you spend a lot of time with her?"

"Actually, I did. While you were dancing." He spun his empty glass around slowly, looking at it then finally raised his gaze. "Trust me. She's not the one for you."

"Why's that, Gid?"

"Because she's the one for me."

Chapter Ten

It took Tricia a minute to adjust to waking up in her own bed again the next morning. No sunrise greeted her through a big picture window like at Noah's. Here her room was small, although not oppressive by any means. She'd grown up in this house and hadn't thought much about its size until she'd moved into Noah's huge place.

Her house was an early-1900s, two-bedroom, one-bath craftsman, with shingled siding and a wide front porch. His was built in the past decade and was a mansion—the only word that could describe it, even with its rustic wood-and-rock exterior.

She loved her cozy home and all its wonderful memories, would miss it when she moved away.

But change is good, she reminded herself. The new adventure would lead her to an entirely new environment, close to the ocean, a different, more laid-back lifestyle, yet still in a city, where she felt most comfortable. She would buy a bicycle and explore. Maybe get a dog. She hadn't had a dog since she was a kid.

Tricia made her way to the kitchen to brew some coffee, her head aching from her champagne overindulgence. Caffeine would help. Normally she sat at the kitchen table with her coffee and newspaper on Sunday morning, but she'd canceled the paper, being home only one morning a week now. Since she had no car, she couldn't go get a paper, so she showered away last night's party instead, then dressed in old jeans and a T-shirt and started peeling wallpaper from her mother's bedroom walls.

She'd been avoiding thinking about Noah, but doing a few hours of the mindless work left her thoughts free to wander. Seeing him last night at the bar, away from his normal environment, gave her a new look at him. He'd been more relaxed, had even laughed out loud. He'd been dressed similarly to her—in boots, jeans and a white shirt. The boots added height to his already tall frame, but since her heels were just as high, they were still well matched on the dance floor.

The dance floor. Being held by him. Her pulse pounded at the memory. He was a stunning, imposing man to start with, and the feel of him close to her had made her tingle everywhere. Heat up everywhere. Sizzle…

Oh, yeah, he'd dressed down well.

She was pleased, too, that he'd responded to her shock that his kids hadn't ridden in a limo, even though his company built them, an oversight of Noah's she'd discovered as the kids had streamed out of the house when the party limo arrived to get her. The children were wide-eyed, even the usually unimpressed Zoe.

Yes, Noah was coming around to his role as father, getting more involved, seeing the light. Tricia was proud to have had something to do with that. Just think what more time would do. She could leave happy, knowing that she'd done what she could to bring them together as a family again.

Happy. Tricia ran her scraper up the wall, peeling away a strip of wallpaper. *Would* she be happy? Maybe not that, exactly, but satisfied that she'd been able to help.

Oh, who was she kidding? It was going to be hard to leave. Horribly hard, even moving on to a new, exciting job in a new, stimulating city.

At least he hadn't been trying to convince her to stay on. That would've made things even harder. There was no way she couldn't show up for her new job. She was committed.

Which reminded Tricia that she hadn't heard from her friend Jennifer, whose job she was taking, since Tricia had left a message last week about her new phone number. Tricia hoped Jennifer was all right. She'd had an easy pregnancy so far.

The phone rang. It was only two o'clock. Too early—

"It's Noah," he said, like she wouldn't recognize his voice. "How's it going?"

"It's going." She was hours from being ready to be picked up. "What's up?"

"The Falcon family would like to come help you. It was Zach's idea, but we all agreed. We can sand, strip paper, whatever you need. Then we'll spring for pizza before we head up the hill. What do you think?"

Touched, Tricia sank to the floor. "It would be wonderful of you to help. I could really use it. Thanks."

"Good. Go open your front door and let us in."

She laughed and hung up. Pretty sure of yourself, Noah Falcon.

She wanted to take a minute to clean up a little, but she went straight to the front door. Noah stood in the middle, his brood gathered around him.

"Hi, Miss Tricia," Zach said, grinning ear to ear. "We came to help!"

"And I am so grateful to you. All of you. Please come in."

Zach hugged her, as did Ashley. Adam flew past. Zoe

followed more slowly, looking in every direction, taking it all in. Then Tricia finally let herself look at Noah.

"Bit of a headache this morning?" he asked, his eyes shining.

"A tiny one. The questionable reward of not being the designated driver. Please, come in." She almost reached for him, almost hugged him hello, but caught herself just in time. He was in jeans again, and a T-shirt that showed off his chest and shoulders.

"Nice," he said, looking around then focusing squarely on her. "Good bones. Great architecture."

"It's a mess at the moment."

"Oh, we're talking about the *house,*" he said lightly, surprising her.

Was he flirting? she wondered.

"Renovating is messy," he said. "So, what can we do?"

Everyone took jobs based on their skills and interests. Zoe worked with Noah on the kitchen cabinets, using a small hand sander to rough up the old paint to accept new. Adam used sandpaper to do the crevices that the flat sander couldn't reach. Zach helped Tricia strip wallpaper. And Ashley was everywhere, cleaning up after everyone. She gathered old wallpaper to put in the trash and vacuumed sandpaper dust constantly, so much, in fact, that a frustrated Zoe yelled at her to stop getting in the way.

Tricia peeked into the kitchen at the surprising outburst. Ashley started to cry. Zoe looked miserable. Adam kept sanding away, music blasting through his earbuds, keeping him unaware. Zach had stayed in the bedroom.

Tricia exchanged a glance with Noah. That was all. Just one glance.

"What do you think, Miss Tricia?" Noah said, reading her exactly. "Time to break for dinner?"

"Absolutely. I'm starving. I'll call in the pizza order. What does everyone like?"

They settled on two different kinds. The kids went into the backyard to play and unwind while Tricia and Noah finished the cabinets and cleaned up, getting everything ready for the painter to come the next day.

"This helped so much," she said when they were done.

"Zach's idea, as I said. It's interesting seeing where you live."

"How did they like the limo ride?"

"Adam insists I bring one home and hire a chauffeur. He says the family should be the official product testers. Where'd he come up with that phrase, do you suppose?"

"Your kids are smart, Noah. Good luck when they hit their teens."

"That's only a couple of months away for the girls."

She smiled sympathetically.

"How do you do it?" he asked.

"Do what?"

"Be so at ease with them. I don't know how to talk to them."

She figured it was a huge admission for him to make. "You seem to be doing okay."

"They're stiff with me. They don't say much in our nightly talks in my office, although it's better than it used to be."

Tricia shoved the last box out of the way, the kitchen finally straightened up. "Take them on dates."

"What?"

"Do something one-on-one with each of them, something they like. They'll open up." She wandered over to where he stood watching them play tag in the backyard.

"It's that simple?"

"It's a start. Just keep at it." Their arms were almost touching. She felt heat, tempting, exciting.

"I probably wasn't the most interactive dad to start with, but since Margie died, I pulled away more. It should've drawn us together. Closer."

"There was a disconnect with my mom and me, too, when my dad died. Losing someone you love so much isn't something you can prepare for. No one knows how they'll react. What matters is what's happening now." She put her hand on his back, needing to touch him, to offer comfort, but also to just connect with him.

He faced her, his gaze intense, his jaw set. "You're very wise."

"It's easy to give advice to someone else." She rubbed his back. He closed his eyes and made a soft, low sound. After a minute, he turned his head and looked at her, his gaze intense, his jaw taut. A second later he eased away and went outside to join his children.

The pizza arrived. Everyone crowded around her dining room table, elbowing each other, shoveling pizza down as if they hadn't eaten in years.

"Who's that, Miss Tricia?" Zach asked, pointing to a framed photo inside a box of others she'd taken down.

"That's my mother and father."

Adam scrutinized it. "They're too young."

She smiled. "That picture was taken twenty-three years ago."

"Where do they live?" Zach asked.

"My mom passed away last year. My dad died when I was eleven."

Silence filled the room, then finally Zach said, "You're all alone?"

"I have a grandpa and some aunts and uncles and cousins, but none of them live around here."

"And you have us," Ashley said, patting her hand.

The simple gesture and surety of her words touched Tricia's heart. Why hadn't Noah told them she was leaving? They needed not to be so invested emotionally in her—nor she in them.

"You don't have any brothers or sisters?" Zoe asked, the first time she'd gotten personal with Tricia.

"No. I always wished I did. You're all very lucky to have

each other." She hadn't looked at Noah during the exchange, but she felt his interest, his sympathy.

"How come you're fixing up your house?" Adam asked, trying to stuff a long string of cheese in his mouth.

"It was time for a spruce-up."

"She's going to sell it," Zoe said, challenging Tricia with her eyes. "I saw the papers."

"Snooping's wrong," Ashley said, chiding her sister.

"I didn't snoop. They were on the dining room table, right out in the open. Miss Tricia put them away."

"Are you coming to live with us all the time?" Zach asked. Every gaze trained on her.

"No, I'm still going to have weekends off."

Noah stood. "It's time to head up the hill. Do you have everything you need?" he asked Tricia.

"Everything except my guitar." She looked at Adam. "It's in my bedroom. Do you want to get it?"

Adam raced off, and the girls followed, then Noah left, after throwing out the trash. Tricia grabbed a couple of things from her closet. She double-checked that the windows were closed and locked. Zach was waiting by the front door for her.

"Did you forget something?" she asked.

"No. I wanted to give you a hug."

"You did?" She knelt. He went into her arms and squeezed her tight. Her eyes welled. "Thank you so much, Zach. How did you know I needed a hug?"

"I miss my mom a whole lot, but you don't have a mom *or* a dad."

He really was the kindest, sweetest little boy she'd ever met. She framed his face with her hands and kissed his cheek. "Thank you," she managed to say.

"I have lots of hugs. Whenever you want one, just tell me, okay?"

"Deal. You do the same. I wish I'd met your mom, Zach."

"Me, too."

They walked hand-in-hand to the car. Noah looked curiously at them but didn't ask any questions until they got home and the kids all took off to the family room.

"Everything okay with you and Zach?" Noah asked before she could head up to her own room. She intended to take a long, hot bath in the spa tub, then go to bed early.

"He's a sweetheart. It really bothers him that I don't have a mom or dad." She'd found a special bond with all of the children today because of their shared losses, a bond she wished they didn't have, but a fact of life.

Noah stared at her oddly, intently.

"What's wrong?" she asked.

"That's my question."

"What do you mean?"

"What's wrong with you, Tricia McBride? How can anyone be so perfect?"

"You're crazy. I'm not perfect. Far from it."

"Really?" He leaned an arm on the newel post and smiled at her. "What do you think your flaws are?"

She ticked them off on her fingers. "I can barely cook. I'm not diplomatic all the time. I used to be comfortable with routine, then when I decided to shake things up, I swung too far the other way, so now I'm impatient."

"Not with the kids."

"No. With myself. If you'd known me before, you would see the change in me."

"What do you think my flaws are?" he asked.

"Oh, no. Uh-uh. You have to say them yourself."

"But I'm interested in what you see."

She smiled. "I wouldn't presume to say. You're my boss."

"I don't feel like your boss."

The discussion was getting way too serious for her. "That's *your* problem," she said with a grin.

"Not necessarily. You don't let me be boss."

"Life's short—"

"Dad!" Zach came running from the family room, skidding to a halt next to Noah. "Tell them *everyone* has to say yes."

"To what?"

"They all want to watch the video of Mom. I don't. Tell them no."

Tricia could see how torn Noah was—and she was partly responsible for the problem. Talking about her parents' deaths had probably spurred the interest. "If it's all right with you, Noah," she said, "Zach and I could do something else for now."

Relief settled in Noah's eyes. "Works for me. How about you, Zachary?"

He nodded.

"Come on," Tricia said, holding out her hand to the boy. "What would you like to do?"

Noah mouthed a thank you as they started up the stairs. She smiled back.

"I want to play chess," Zach said.

Great. "I've never played chess."

"I meant on the computer."

Nine years old and a chess aficionado already. Tricia wondered if Zach would be the one to cure cancer or something else equally significant. He seemed destined for greatness.

Tricia sat next to him and was given a lesson in the game of chess. It amazed her how he could look three moves ahead.

"Miss Tricia?" he said when the match ended. "Do you remember your dad?"

She laid an arm on the back of his chair. "Yes."

"Like what kinds of things?"

"He smoked a pipe, so I remember how that smelled. When

I'm out someplace and I smell pipe tobacco, I always think of my dad. And he wore plaid shorts, a white undershirt and hiking boots when he mowed the lawn. Always the same thing. And he kept his car spotless. Oh, and he loved fried chicken. It's one of the few things I can cook well."

"Was he nice?"

"Very nice." She paused to let him direct the conversation.

"My dad used to go to Europe a lot. Mom would let us all get in bed with her sometimes and watch television and eat popcorn. And she made the best chocolate cake in the whole world."

Jealousy nipped at Tricia. Noah had been married to a saint. No wonder he was still grieving. He probably found flaws in every woman he met.

Except you, she reminded herself. He thought she was perfect, which was dangerous thinking. She didn't want to be put on anyone's pedestal.

The sound of him climbing the staircase stopped further conversation. He appeared at the top. He seemed to have aged years in the past hour.

"Time for bed, son."

"Okay," Zach said, moving toward the stairs.

"You doing okay?" Noah asked him.

"I won."

Noah didn't say anything for a few seconds, then he squeezed Zach's shoulder. "Good for you."

"Will you tuck us in?"

"Be there in ten minutes."

"You, too, Miss Tricia?"

"Sure thing. Thanks for the lesson."

"You're welcome." He hurried off.

Noah came all the way into the room. He slipped his hands in his pockets. "Thanks. I know you should be off duty."

"This was more important." She met him midway. "How'd the kids do?"

"Ashley cried. Zoe never said anything. Adam was surprising. He was the only one to laugh." The lines on his face deepened.

Sympathetic, she laid her hands on his shoulders. He stiffened, then settled a little—just a little. Like earlier today, she had no business touching him, but their shared losses were a bond she couldn't ignore. "I'm so sorry, Noah. I know how much you must miss her."

After a long, emotion-escalating moment, he drew her into his arms and held her. She held him back, hard, then he completely enfolded her, pressing his face into her shoulder, a quiet moan escaping him.

Oh, but it felt wonderful to be held again, especially by this man. She'd been drawn to him from the moment she'd seen him walk into the girls' bedroom. The initial part of his appeal was physical, then had grown from there, way too fast. She was walking a tightrope, had thrown away her own safety net by touching him, holding him.

She made no effort to move away, enjoying his heat and scent and need.

Finally he straightened. He cupped her head, his fingers threading through her curls to lie against her scalp. Would he kiss her? Could she let him?

He defused the situation himself, dropping his hands, moving back. He looked bewildered.

"Thanks. I needed that," she said lightly, making it seem like she was the only one in need. "Talking about my parents today was hard."

"Sure. No problem." He glanced at his watch, then hitched a thumb toward the stairs. "Time to tuck them in."

"You take the boys first and I'll take the girls?"

He nodded.

They passed each other in the hall as they changed rooms, then met in the middle again in a few minutes.

"Thanks again for all the help today," she said. "One more thing I can cross off my list. Now comes the big, brave moment when I actually put the For Sale sign up. Talk about shaking up my life. Although not as big a shake-up as taking the job in San Diego, I guess."

"When did you work in San Diego?"

Tricia stared at him. She put a hand to her mouth as awareness sank in. "He didn't tell you."

"Who didn't tell me what?"

"David. He didn't tell you my plans."

"What plans?"

"Noah, I've accepted a job in San Diego that starts in January. My dream job. Working for you is only temporary, has always been temporary, to give you time to hire the right person this time. Someone who'll stay."

Her throat burned at the look on his face—shock, then anger, escalating to fury.

"I had no idea you didn't know. I'm so sorry, Noah."

"You never talked about leaving." His jaw seemed locked.

"And I kept wondering why you never brought it up. I never hid it. You knew from the beginning that I was selling my house and never questioned me about it."

He tunneled his fingers through his hair. "I assumed you had your own place, that you were just selling your mother's house."

"I'd been taking care of her for four years, then traveled for a year," she said gently, seeing how staggered he was. "Why would I have lived someplace else?"

"I don't know. I didn't think about it."

"The night I moved in here you asked if my room was okay, and I said it was fine, that my time here would be limited, anyway."

He blew out a breath. "I thought you meant because you wouldn't be here on weekends."

She admired the way he pulled himself together, could see the CEO, man-in-charge in him. She wondered what would change now. He would have to tell the children. She didn't want to think about how that would change things between them, too.

"I need to go out," he said. "You'll watch the kids?"

"Of course. Noah…" She put a hand on his arm, which was as rigid as steel. "I'm so sorry," she said again.

He nodded then turned away.

All she could do was wait.

Chapter Eleven

Fifteen minutes later, Noah pulled into David's driveway. He hadn't cooled down by even one degree. He'd made the drive to David's, forcing himself to go the speed limit, gripping the wheel so hard his hands cramped.

He climbed the back stairs and rapped on the kitchen door. "Hey!"

Noah turned around at the sound of David's voice coming from behind him.

"We're in the cottage. Come join us."

"I need to talk to you. Alone."

"Okay. I'll tell Valerie and be right there. It's unlocked."

Noah went into the house and headed for the living room. He had to walk past a wall of photos on his way, so he stopped there, knowing he couldn't sit. There were several shots of the three brothers at various ages. Pictures of David's mother, June, whom Noah remembered more than his own.

And one of their father, alone, in front of the first car he'd designed and built.

Falcon Motorcars may have been created by Aaron Falcon, but it was the successful company it was today because of David and Noah. Gideon had bowed out of the business a long time ago.

"I had a talk with him the other night," David said from behind him. "Dad, I mean. Told him how much he'd messed me up. Didn't forgive him, either, just chalked it up to experience and moved forward."

"You've got some of his traits."

"Like hell I do."

The brothers squared off. "Everything he did that hurt us in some way, he'd justify it by saying it was for our own good," Noah said.

"I remember. What's that got to do with me?"

"What's that got—? You didn't think it was important that I knew Tricia was only temporary?"

"Ah. She told you."

"It came up in conversation. She thought I knew. What the hell were you thinking, controlling my life like that? Controlling my children's lives. Once again, they're set up to be hurt. This time even more, probably, because they've already bonded with her. Having her leave is going to destroy them."

"Then you need to do something about it."

The volcano of Noah's anger roiled, ready to spew. "Who are you to—"

"Your brother," David interrupted before Noah could get going. "Which gives me rights."

"Not when it causes pain for my children, it doesn't."

"I'm their uncle. I love them. What I did, I did for them as much as you." He set a hand on Noah's shoulder. "Let's sit down. Have a beer."

He shrugged off David's hand. "I'll pass."

David sighed. "Okay, then. Here's what I did and why. When Jessica told Valerie she was going to quit, I knew you'd handle it the way you always do—hire someone fresh out of college who doesn't really understand what she's getting into. Like how isolated she would be. How you would expect her to be a nanny, not just a teacher, available all the time. Someone who wouldn't stand up to you. So, I got busy. I found you the best person I could in the short amount of time I had."

"Who already has another job lined up," Noah said. "And who also hates the country, by the way."

"All you have to do is convince her to stay."

"Oh, sure, simple. She called the job she's going to her dream job."

"Noah, the woman already adores your children. I could tell when we were there for dinner, and she'd barely had a chance to know them yet. Your kids are doing *their* part just by being themselves. It's up to you to do your part."

Noah was completely bewildered. "Which is what?"

"Woo her."

"She's my employee." Should he admit he'd imagined her in his bed? Had dreamed about her naked and rolling around with him, her hands and mouth touching him everywhere? Him touching her everywhere?

"Valerie was my employee," David said. "Worked out just fine."

"I'm not looking for a wife. I just want a teacher who'll stay. I want my children to have stability."

"They get their stability from you, Noah, because you are the one thing in their lives that never changes. And, just so we're clear, I wasn't looking for a wife, either. Anyway, I'm talking about being good to Tricia, receptive to her ideas, open to debate, giving her time off when she wants it. I'm talking about wooing her as an employee. Although if something else should happen…"

"If by 'something else' you mean have a physical relationship with her, you know I can't. I can't keep her as the children's teacher *and* be sleeping with her. That's certain disaster." He walked away, needing to move. "And I'm not getting married again. At least not until the kids are grown. I won't put them through that kind of potential loss again. It's been too hard. A second time? Can't do it."

His tension ebbed slightly. David's idea was good. Do whatever it takes to keep Tricia.

Get her to see that being their teacher was her dream job. The idea presented itself in neon in his mind.

"Keep your eye on the prize," David said. "You especially need to be open to change, which you know is one of your problems. Status quo makes you very happy."

"There's nothing wrong with status quo."

David only laughed.

"Why didn't you tell me?" Noah asked.

"Because you would've dismissed her out of hand. I knew she was the right one." David cocked his head. "Didn't take too long for you to see that, either. And you're welcome, by the way."

"You've totally complicated my life, and I'm supposed to thank you? I may never speak to you again."

David only smiled. "That could make my life at work a whole lot easier."

Reluctantly, so did Noah. "I think I'll take you up on that beer now."

"Everyone needs to shake their lives up now and then, you know." David took a couple of steps backward. "I'll let Valerie know I won't be back tonight, get my good-night kiss."

"You don't sleep together?"

"Not until we're married—at night anyway," he added with a wink. "Hannah may only be eight, but she notices everything. We can wait a few more days. Be right back."

Shake up your life. It seemed to have become his life quote—according to everyone else.

Noah wandered back to the wall of photos. There were a few things he wanted to say to their father, too. If he were alive, Noah would make him stand there and take it like a man. He'd bullied all three of his sons, had gotten sole custody of each of them by bullying their mothers, effectively destroying the mother/son relationships, too. Only Gideon had reconnected well as an adult.

Status quo makes you very happy. David's words rang in his head. Status quo had not been his father's contentment barometer. He'd needed the adrenaline rush of risk, and also constant change. Maybe Noah *had* gone to extremes to be unlike his father. Demanded too much of others, especially his children.

Tricia had forced changes there. The children had responded well.

Noah heard the kitchen door open and close. He couldn't figure out everything in one night. For now, he would toss back a beer with his brother and forget for an hour or two that he was CEO of a thriving international corporation and single father of four.

And a man tempted by a woman he didn't dare touch.

Tricia's bedroom window faced the front of the house, so the only way she would know that Noah had come home was to watch the road through a small forest of trees for his car to approach. She'd pulled up a chair and was waiting. She didn't know where he'd gone. She only knew he was furious. No one should drive anywhere furious.

She didn't want him to fire her. She didn't even want him to find a replacement for her until January. They needed her to stay for a while and continue to help them rediscover each other as a family.

That was a lie. Yes, it was. They could do fine without her. They'd had a good foundation and were on their way again. It hadn't taken much time at all, just someone to help them look at things differently. Noah had been ready for it, without knowing he was ready.

Yes, they would do fine. She, on the other hand, might not, especially as she found herself drawn to Noah more and more.

Finally, at close to midnight, she spotted headlights. She tugged her sweater down, pressed her hands against her stomach and went downstairs. If she were wise, she would probably give him until after work tomorrow, let him think things through. But she couldn't wait that long for her stomach to settle down from the worry.

She encountered him when she reached the bottom stair. He came to a quick halt.

"You waited up?" he asked.

"You know that old adage about not going to bed worried."

"I thought it was never go to sleep angry."

She shrugged. He seemed calm, not furious at all. She wondered where he'd gone and how he'd settled down. A girlfriend, maybe?

"Safe and sound, as you can see," he said. "But thanks for the concern."

She figured she might as well ask the question that would either keep her up all night or let her sleep. "You're okay with me staying on?"

"Yes."

That was it? *Yes?* She would've liked more than that, but she guessed she couldn't push at this point. "Okay, good. I'm glad. See you tomorrow."

She turned to head back upstairs. He cupped her elbow, stopping her, turning her toward him again. "I don't want the kids to know yet. I'll tell them when the time is right."

She had mixed feelings about that. "I don't want to drop a bomb on them right before I leave."

"I won't wait that long."

She wanted to kiss him, ached to kiss him. And be held by him, her head against his broad shoulder, his strong arms wrapped around her. It'd been so long. So very long…

He rubbed his thumb above her elbow. On purpose? Now that he knew she was temporary, was it going to change their relationship? Would he act on the attraction she could see was mutual?

"Good night, Tricia."

She forced a smile. "'Night." She headed up the stairs, knowing he was watching her, not swaying her hips as she had once, but aware of the fact he hadn't moved.

She made it to her room then dropped onto her bed, covering her eyes with her hands. She hadn't felt that kind of pull toward a man since…since Darrell, and he'd died more than ten years ago. She'd been attracted to a few men since then, but nothing like this.

Now what?

Maybe she should leave, after all. Maybe she should tell him to find her replacement right now, and she could go back to Sacramento, finish up the work on the house and take off for San Diego as soon as it sold. She would have a little money to live on from the sale, could find a place to rent and get to know the area before she reported for work. Spend extra time with Jennifer, whose job Tricia would be taking. The learning curve would be huge.

Although when Tricia had finally reconnected with Jennifer, her friend hadn't encouraged Tricia to come to San Diego early.

Except for Jennifer, she'd let most of her friendships die since she put her life on hold to care for her mother and then take the time to travel and heal. It wasn't as if she had reasons to stay on in Sacramento for any length of time.

Tricia dragged a pillow onto her chest and hugged it. She'd lived with regrets for a long time. She was done with living with regrets, had promised herself never to pass up an opportunity again, to take the road to adventure whenever it presented itself.

She wanted to stay for the time she'd agreed to. Wanted to be with Noah and his children. Wanted to see them come full circle.

That was it, then. Decision made. She would stay for now. If Noah hired a new teacher next week, she wouldn't be leaving out of her choice but his, so she wouldn't have anything to feel guilty about.

Hugely relieved at having made her decision, Tricia got ready for bed, turned out the light and climbed under the blankets. Knowing Noah was doing the same thing at the other end of the long hall comforted her—and excited her.

Tomorrow things would return to normal. Whatever happened, happened. For now, she had a plan.

Chapter Twelve

Noah didn't like to be kept waiting. Cynthia was supposed to meet him at the Lode at eight o'clock, and it was now ten minutes after.

It was Tuesday, two nights since he'd held Tricia in his arms. Since he'd learned she planned to leave.

Two nights since he hadn't corrected her when she said she knew how much Noah missed Margie. Guilt ate at him for not telling her the truth.

He'd watched the clips of his late wife with Ashley clinging to him, squeezing painfully now and then. He'd kept an eye on Zoe, who was too quiet, too controlled. Adam had been fully engaged, but then he'd been six when Margie died. His memories weren't as strong or detailed as his sisters'—or Noah's.

And seeing Margie talking and walking and laughing, holding the children as babies, playing with them as toddlers, and all the events that followed, hadn't crushed him like they used to. He missed her, but not with the day-to-day ache hovering over him like a black cloud, the way it used to.

How much of that was because of Tricia? He figured he'd been inching toward recovery, but the embrace he'd shared with her had seemed to catapult him further.

She'd felt amazing in his arms, fitting perfectly, her body as strong and curvy as he'd imagined. She'd also tried to make it seem as if she'd been the only one to need the hug, when they both knew his need was as powerful as hers, maybe even more so.

Noah spun the salt and pepper shakers on the tabletop, flipped through the song list on the mini jukebox.

The diner door opened, and Cynthia hurried in. Not counting Halloween, the only times he'd seen her away from his house had been for business reasons, so he was surprised to see her wearing a definitely unbusinesslike low-cut sweater and second-skin jeans.

He stood to greet her.

"I'm so sorry I'm late," she said, her long red hair down and flowing, curls drifting over her breasts, which seemed to be pushed up and in. "I'm meeting someone after this, and my last evaluation with a family ran over. I tried to call and let you know but my cell had died."

She hugged him, as if that was something they always did. Her perfume transferred to him, clinging, filling his head, even when they sat on opposite sides of the table.

Having just watched the video of Margie, he realized how much Cynthia resembled her. Red hair, although a different shade, quick smile, and a petite but sexy body.

"Am I forgiven?" she asked when he didn't say anything.

"No problem. I hadn't ordered yet. What would you like?"

"They make wonderful hot fudge sundaes here. Of course they're way too big. Maybe you'd like to split one?"

That seemed too intimate. "I'd decided on lemon pie, but thanks."

She ended up ordering apple pie.

"So, you said you have some concerns," he said, wanting to get the business going.

She leaned her elbows on the table. "I've noticed some changes in the children for a while now. I'm a little worried about them."

"In what way?"

"They stopped pushing themselves to excel. They seem to do the bare-bones requirements but nothing more."

"Even Ashley and Zach?"

"Yes."

He was annoyed that she hadn't said anything until now.

"I had been working more closely with Jessica to improve the situation," she said. "I was stunned when she left. She didn't tell me she was quitting."

"Me, either. She told my brother David. He hired Tricia for me." The waitress brought their pies and coffees, which forced Cynthia to sit up straight, for which Noah was grateful. "What do you think is the problem with my children?"

"Boredom. Sameness. Getting older, especially the girls, which brings about personality changes. Frankly, Noah, none of the teachers you've hired have inspired the children very much. They were competent, and the children liked them, but that was all."

He knew that. As David had explained, they hadn't had enough experience, being fresh out of college. And they weren't happy in the remote location. Or with him. He was doing his best to change that now. "Tricia has experience."

"Only with kindergarteners, and that was six years ago."

"Does that matter?"

"It can. That's why I decided to work very closely with her, rather than it getting away from us this time. We can make adjustments early on."

"That sounds like a good idea." He took a bite of pie, enjoying the tangy lemon flavor balanced by the sweet meringue.

"I'm glad you agree. Would you talk to Tricia about getting on the same page with me, then?"

"You mean you talked to her, and she isn't cooperating?" He had a hard time picturing her being uncooperative about anything to do with the kids. "Did she tell you why?"

"She wants to see what she can do first."

"That makes sense to me, Cynthia."

"She's new at being a homeschool teacher. I've had eight years of experience in the field. She should listen to me, don't you think?"

Noah would have openly agreed with Tricia that she be allowed the opportunity to find her own path to success with the kids, except that she didn't intend to stay—unless he could convince her otherwise. And time was wasting on that front.

"What I've observed," he said instead, "is that the kids have become very engaged with their studies under Tricia's tutelage. She's making them stretch. She gets them outdoors a lot more than any of the other teachers did. Maybe you should reserve judgment until the next time you come. Let her settle in."

She mulled that over for a minute. "I'll do whatever you say, of course."

"Don't think I don't appreciate your concern or suggestions, Cynthia. Or that I don't value your expertise. I realize we've been through a lot of teachers, but I've also come to realize why, so I'm trying to make adjustments myself. I want consistency for my children, too."

"So, you think she'll be the one who'll stay?"

"I'm doing my best to assure that happens." Noah eyed her curiously. So far, they hadn't discussed anything they couldn't have dealt with over the phone.

She set her fork down and picked up her coffee mug. Before

she took a sip, she said, "I know this is going to sound strange coming from me, but maybe it's time you seriously consider public school."

Strange wasn't the word. Shocking, maybe. "Why?"

"We both know it was Margie's passion to homeschool them, not yours. It's been very difficult for you to continue. I understand why you wanted to keep the status quo for them in the beginning, but given the problems you've come up against, I think you'd find more consistency for them in public school. Or even in private schools, if you'd prefer, although they'd have a longer commute each day." She reached across the table and covered his hand with hers. "You've made an incredible effort, Noah. But maybe enough's enough."

He pulled his hand free. Her words had the opposite effect from what she'd intended. It made him dig his heels in further to convince Tricia to stay. He wanted Margie's legacy continued. He believed she would've approved of Tricia and her approach to education. He knew his children already did.

He picked up his mug. "I'm not ready to do that."

"I just wanted to plant the idea. I apologize if I overstepped."

They ate in silence for a little while. He liked Cynthia, always had. He thought she had a good head on her shoulders, and stayed focused on the goal. *Had* she overstepped? She was a critical part of his children's success. If she couldn't talk to him honestly, who could?

"I do appreciate your input," he said to her. "I'll keep a closer eye on what's happening at home. If I see a problem before you're due for their monthly evaluation, I'll have you come sooner. We can revisit this at another time."

"That's fine." She glanced at her watch. "I need to get going."

"I'll walk you to your car." He dropped some bills on the table and followed her out the door. She drove a van large enough to be a mobile office. "Do you like your work?" he asked.

"I love my work. I love children. If I weren't doing this, I'd be teaching." She cocked her head. "Do you like *your* work?"

He nodded. "Everything about it."

She glanced at the Falcon sports car he'd driven, parked ahead of hers. It was too cold to have the top down, which always made him feel hemmed in.

"So, when is Falcon Motorcars going to make a van that doesn't make a thirty-two-year-old single woman look like a soccer mom?" Cynthia asked. "If anyone can redesign the van to appeal to that market, it would be you."

"I'll pass along the idea, but don't hold your breath."

She grinned, then did just that, drawing in a deep breath, making her breasts seem ready to pop out of her sweater.

"We'll be in touch," he said then headed for his car. He waited until she'd pulled away, then he pulled out his cell phone, hit a speed-dial number.

"You free?" Noah asked.

"No, but I'm reasonable."

Noah laughed. "I'll be there in ten."

The house was quiet when Noah got home, not surprising, since it was midnight. He turned off the pendant light over the kitchen sink, which Tricia must have left on for him, then he followed a light trail through the dining room to the staircase. He stopped whistling when he heard the sound echo in the house. He hadn't been aware he *was* whistling.

He felt better than he had in a while, more sure of what he must do in order to keep his life moving in an orderly fashion and his children happy.

He climbed two steps at a time, got halfway up the staircase, then looked down and spotted Tricia curled up in an oversize chair in the living room. She hadn't said a word. Hadn't alerted him in any way that she was there. Guilt snaked through him that he hadn't called to let her know he would be later than he'd expected. She was supposed to be off the clock, after all, yet he'd needed her to watch the kids so that he could meet with Cynthia.

Then he'd taken advantage by going elsewhere and staying late, figuring the kids would be asleep anyway.

He went back down the stairs and approached Tricia.

"Hi," she said. "How did your meeting go?"

"It was fine. What's going on? Why are you down here?" She wasn't dressed for bed but wore jeans and a sweater.

"I heard a wolf. Or a coyote. How do you tell the difference? And then I saw something large and black. It raced across the driveway." Fear made her voice tight, raising it an octave.

He noted how tightly she hugged herself. He was pretty sure if he turned on a light, her face would be ashen. For a woman who otherwise always seemed in control, it was strange to see her fear. And kind of endearing. "We don't have wolves, and rarely a coyote. Plus, you're indoors, Tricia."

"It wasn't the only noise I heard."

He put his hands on her arms and rubbed them. "What else did you hear?"

"I don't know. Something below my bedroom window. Banging." She closed her eyes. "I hate that you're seeing me like this."

He wasn't sorry. He could use all the insight he could get so that he knew how to deal with her. "Fear can be irrational, Tricia, and your particular fear is closer to a phobia. Give yourself a break."

"I feel so childish."

"When was the last time you heard the banging?" he asked, diverting the conversation.

"An hour ago, when I was getting ready for bed."

He held out his hand. "I'll go to your room with you and check it out. If we can identify it, will you be able to sleep?"

"I'll sleep now anyway, because you're home."

He liked that. "Humor me."

He wondered if she would accept his hand, accept his help. She did, not letting go until they reached her room.

They stood just inside the door, listening.

"That?" he asked.

"No, I recognize that. It's branches from the tree outside. I've already asked Joseph to trim— There. That."

He couldn't identify it, either. "I'll check it out. Do you want to stay or come?"

She hesitated. "I'll go with you."

He didn't take her hand again until they'd put on jackets and he'd grabbed a flashlight. They had to walk down the driveway, around the back of the house, across where Joseph had tilled the land for the putting green. As they made the turn along the side of the house, she pulled herself closer to him.

Was it totally chauvinistic of him to be enjoying her fear? To be feeling protective of her? It really should just have been a reminder that she wasn't cut out for living here, for staying on. Conquering that much fear seemed like a big, uphill climb.

Something banged against the rock trim that lined the lower six feet of the house. Tricia not only squeezed his hand harder, she grabbed his arm, as well. He turned his flashlight toward the sound. A large crate the kids used to store their outdoor equipment was turned upside down, sporting gear scattered around it. Something was inside, trying to get out.

"What *is* that?" Tricia asked.

"Skunk, probably."

She let out a small shriek and took off backward. He laughed. "I'm kidding. A skunk couldn't move a crate that size."

She heaved a breath. "You brat."

"Sue me." He knelt, shining his light inside. The crate began to move again, accompanied by grunts. "Bear."

"A bear? You have bears?" Fear shifted to panic in her voice.

"No. Sorry. Bear is the name of a dog from up the road. He does a lot of night traveling. He also howls. It's eerie. That's probably what you heard."

"Why haven't I heard him before now?"

"His owners try to keep him penned up at night, but he's a regular Houdini." Noah grabbed hold of the temporary prison. Bear jumped and wriggled, making the crate move. As soon as he was freed, he took off, almost knocking both of them down on his way.

"Not much of a people dog," Noah said as he righted the crate.

They dumped the equipment back in. Tricia found the lid propped against the house and eyed it thoughtfully.

"What?" Noah asked.

"Doesn't it seem odd that the lid is way over here?" She asked for the flashlight and started searching the ground.

"What are you looking for?"

"I'll know it when I see it. Ah-ha!" She picked up a slat of wood and groaned. "Adam."

Noah took the slat, noted the small vee-notch carved into one end—the better to keep the crate up. "Why would Adam do this?"

"His science project. They had to do something that involved the outdoors. I gave them a list of possibilities. Obviously Adam chose a project not on the list."

"I doubt he'd expected to trap Bear."

"No, but maybe he *had* intended to lure a skunk. And notice where he put his trap—right under my window."

That didn't make sense to Noah. "Adam likes you."

"Does he? I can't read him well. He seems to go with the flow more than the others, but I'm not sure he isn't hiding his feelings from us, maybe even from himself."

"I'll talk to him tomorrow morning," Noah said.

"How did your meeting with Cynthia go?" she asked as they made their way back into the house.

"It was fine."

"So, what are her concerns?"

"The same as mine. That you're a little unconventional."

A long pause ensued. "Well, you can always hire someone conventional for my replacement."

There was an edge to her voice he hadn't heard before.

"How's that search going, by the way?" she asked.

He felt her gaze bore into him. "I just found out two days ago, you know." His goal to keep her had been reinforced tonight during a long conversation—after watching the Kings game—with Gideon. Noah hadn't wanted to involve him, but David had clued Gid in.

He'd given good advice: "You want the teacher to stay, you have to keep your hands off her."

More than just good advice—solid advice.

It had even seemed feasible—until he'd come home and found her scared and vulnerable. Hell, who was he kidding? He just had to be in the same room for her to have impact.

But the biggest realization he'd come to tonight was that if he didn't do something to distract himself from his attraction to his children's teacher he was going to make a big mistake with her, and she would quit for sure. Maybe sooner than January.

So. Invite someone out to dinner, that was the plan. Not this weekend because of the wedding, but the following one.

Which gave him plenty of time to plan.

Or change his mind.

Chapter Thirteen

The exquisite setting for David and Valerie's wedding was a white clapboard hotel that had survived since the gold-rush days, and recently renovated to all its mid-nineteenth-century glory. All the tables and chairs in the dining room were pushed to the perimeter, forming a circle, then the whole place was decorated with purple and yellow flower arrangements— tabletop centerpieces, garlands, and an arch of yellow roses and tiny purple orchids under which the bride and groom would take their vows.

Tricia admired the simplicity. Even though David could afford big and lavish, he and Valerie had chosen exquisite—and simple—beauty.

Because Noah was best man, Tricia was in charge of the children, who were uncharacteristically quiet. In fact, they'd been quiet for several days. Also polite and cooperative. She missed their little moments of rebellion or glee or antagonizing a sibling.

She wanted to talk to Noah about it, but every night when they sat in his office to discuss the school day, there never seemed to be a good time to bring it up. Because, really, what could she say? Your children behaved too well today? He would laugh.

And then there was the other issue she hadn't dared ask him about—why he'd been gone until midnight after meeting with Cynthia. He'd been completely relaxed when he got home— very un-Noah-like, had even been whistling when he came through the back door. Did he have a woman on the side? Someone his family didn't know about?

Like any other red-blooded male, he must have needs—

"Hi, Tricia. Is there room at your table for me?" Denise Watson, dressed to the nines in a stunning burnt orange silk gown, perched on the chair next to Tricia. "I don't see place cards, and I don't know anyone else here."

"Of course. I don't even know if Noah is supposed to sit here or at a table with the wedding party. Either way, we can make room for you." She introduced Denise to the children, who were sitting quietly, driving her crazy.

"What well-behaved kids," Denise whispered to her. "Are they always this good?"

"Pretty much." She knew she couldn't complain. No one else would understand.

"Really? I must admit I hadn't totally believed David when he said the children weren't a problem for the nannies. Usually you'd think: Four kids? The problem has to be them."

"They're wonderful."

"So, Noah is that difficult?"

"I don't know what he was like before, but he hasn't been difficult with me. In fact, I think he bends over backward to be nice." The lights dimmed. A man sat at a piano. He was the epitome of tall, dark and gorgeous. And brooding. He started to play. Tricia couldn't have identified Mozart from Mendelssohn, but she recognized beauty when she heard it.

After a minute, when the room had settled into silence, he switched seamlessly to another piece as the adorable junior bridesmaid Hannah walked with groomsman Gideon into the center of the circle, followed by maid of honor Dixie and best man Noah. The judge performing the ceremony came in and took his place, followed by David, who stood under the floral arch. All the men looked gorgeous in their tuxes, but especially Noah, whose height and build really filled out the suit, an imposing sight.

He looked like he could save the world single-handedly. She hadn't realized she'd needed—or wanted—a man to protect her, not until he'd been there for her.

And she'd greatly appreciated how he hadn't teased her about her fears, except to lighten the mood when they were outdoors seeking the source of the strange noise. Since then he hadn't brought it up.

The music segued into something Tricia did recognize, the traditional wedding march. Valerie emerged at the edge of the crowd, dressed in a stunning, simple white gown, her mother beside her. They moved into the open circle, then David took a few steps to meet his bride. The ceremony began.

Tricia had been to a few weddings since Darrell died all those years ago. Each time pain and regret had overwhelmed her so that she hadn't heard the vows or the music. This time was different. This time she heard Valerie's nervousness and David's assuredness. She saw the love reflected in their eyes, in the way they touched, and how they leaned toward each other as if pulled together magnetically.

She let her gaze slide over to Noah, whose expression was blank, and then to Gideon, who looked her way. Why? Then she realized he was focused on Denise, who looked right back.

Tricia glanced around the table at each child. Ashley was enraptured. No surprise there. Zoe, surprisingly, sat still, no fidgeting, no rolling her eyes. Zach yawned. As for Adam, he was carrying on a flirtation with a little girl at the next table.

Adam had owned up to setting the trap to try to catch a wild animal, any wild animal, so that they all could study it up close before they let it go. He said he hadn't realized it was under Tricia's window. He'd only meant to put the trap out of sight from the back windows, creating more of a temptation for an animal to explore and find the steak he'd left as a lure. He'd apologized again and again.

Tricia would've preferred he flash his impish grin instead, as if he were only sorry he got caught, which she believed was closer to the truth.

Magical wedding words drew Tricia back to the ceremony: "You may kiss your bride." They were introduced as husband and wife to a huge round of applause from the hundred or so guests. Formal photographs were taken. Food was served.

Gideon came over to say hello, while Noah stayed behind, although each of the children went up to talk to him on their own, which made Tricia happy.

"I think I'll slip out," Denise said after the toasts were made and the cake served. "I'll try to catch David and Valerie to say goodbye."

Tricia didn't want to be left alone. "Would you mind dropping me off at Noah's? I've had enough, too, and he can keep an eye on his children now that the ceremony is over. They're having fun with their friends, anyway."

"I'd be glad to."

Just then the piano player sat down, and Joseph, the official emcee for the evening, picked up a microphone. The entertainment part of the program was about to begin.

"Guess we can't leave during the couple's first dance," Denise said.

Both women sat again, waiting through announcements and introductions—the pianist was Joseph's brother Donovan, who'd come all the way from London to play at David's wedding—then the first dance. Before it ended, Gideon was there, asking Denise to dance.

"I was just leaving," she said, her protest going unheeded as he took her by the hand and headed toward the dance floor.

Tricia smiled at her gesture of helplessness and settled back to wait. Noah invited Ashley to dance, then tried to include Zoe, who shook her head. Tricia wondered if she knew how. A memory of her own father dancing with her snuck in. He'd been such a sweet man, such a kind father.

She let go of the memory and watched Denise and Gideon instead. She was keeping a little distance from him, but the trade-off was that they had to look at each other. Gideon didn't seem to mind. Actually, neither did Denise.

The song changed and so did a lot of the partners, but not Gideon and Denise. Tricia figured she wasn't going to be leaving anytime soon, after all.

Joseph's brother Jake approached her. "I know we only met briefly at the Stompin' Grounds last week, but if I promise not to step on your feet, will you dance with me?"

She smiled and stood. "Are you taking pity on the wallflower?"

"Nope. I've been admiring you all evening."

They got onto the dance floor just as the song changed from fast to slow. It felt strange to Tricia, being in the arms of a man she barely knew. He was taller than Joseph, and more lanky. Contrary to his opening line, he danced very well. "I hear the man who's playing the piano is your brother. I guess I hadn't realized how big your family is," she said.

"Five girls and three boys. The girls are all married, the boys have escaped, so far. The town has begun to call it the McCoy family curse—subtitled, 'The men who don't commit.'"

"Is that why Joseph won't set a date with Dixie?"

"Only Joe can answer that. He sure is unhappy today, though. And she's gotten really good at ignoring him and seeming to have a good time without him."

"It seems to me a relationship that volatile isn't destined for happiness," she said, then regretting she'd opened her mouth.

"In most cases, I would agree. But they're meant for each other. Everyone knows it." He looked past Tricia to something that caught his attention. "Looks like I've stirred up a hornet's nest by asking you to dance."

"What do you mean?"

"Noah's none too happy with me."

Tricia turned around to look. He was dancing with Dixie, but looking at Tricia.

"We have a history," Jake said. "Goes back to high school, when we were always in competition."

"In sports?"

"That, for sure. But academics, too. School politics. Girls."

"And it continues even now? After all these years?"

"Obviously, since here he comes, ready to cut in. You're not…involved with him, are you?"

"Absolutely not." Just in my dreams, she thought.

"Could I call you sometime?"

Tricia had the feeling that it was the competition that piqued his interest, since he asked loudly enough that Noah couldn't miss hearing it.

He clamped a hand on Jake's shoulder. "Dixie wants to talk to you. It's important."

Jake gave Tricia a slight smile. "I'll track you down later, if you don't mind."

"I don't mind." The words had barely been spoken before

she was in Noah's arms. This time he pulled her closer than he had at the party last weekend.

"He's a ladies' man," Noah said. "Be careful."

And exactly who were you with until midnight Tuesday? She wondered. Who exactly *is* the ladies man? "I'm not looking for someone for the long haul. Not in Chance City."

His hold on her tightened. Where was the relaxed Noah she'd seen all week? Was his competition with Jake that fierce?

"I'm no one's pawn, Noah. Don't put me in the middle of your feud. And if you continue to hold me like this, everyone is going to jump to conclusions about us."

He loosened his grip. "So, he told you."

"Not in any detail, but enough that I know there is a game of one-upsmanship between you that should've ended in high school but continues almost twenty years later."

"Maybe you shouldn't be so quick to criticize when you don't know the whole story."

"What does that mean, Noah?"

The piano equivalent of a drum roll resounded, then Joseph spoke. "Okay, all you single ladies. Time to catch the bouquet. Gather over here, please."

No one came forward.

"Don't be shy now."

Still no one.

"Why aren't you going over there?" Noah asked.

"I don't want to be the next one to get married. I've got some things to accomplish first."

"You mean you believe in the myth of the bouquet catch?"

"Of course I do."

He smiled and shook his head. "Every time I think I have a handle on you, you throw me for a loop."

"Is that bad?"

"Could be."

"Okay," Joseph said, "I see I have to take charge. Hometown beauty queen and fearsome lawyer Laura Bannister, get up here."

"Don't want to get leg-shackled, Joseph!" she called back. "Tricia McBride!"

"No ticking clock here!" she shouted back—a lie, since she did want to get married and have a family, but she wasn't about to stand up there by herself. She was an outsider.

"Denise Watson!"

"I'd sooner swim across Lake Tahoe in the winter."

He named all the single women except Dixie, the exclusion blatant. It took Valerie pretending to cry to get the women huddled on the floor, without Dixie, who Tricia believed would ordinarily have put herself front and center.

Valerie turned around. Quiet descended. She tossed the bouquet in the air but not at the women waiting. Instead she fired it at Dixie, who caught it reflexively, then, as if it were on fire, pitched it at the group of women, hitting Tricia in the face.

She held on tight as people hooted and hollered, although just as much at Dixie as at her.

Tricia buried her face in the white-rose-and-orchid bouquet, inhaling the sweet scent, the fragrance a sudden, sharp reminder of her own lost love. They'd decided on white roses, too.

Regret laid her low in an instant. If Darrell had lived, she would've had her own family now, a husband to sleep beside, to lean on, like she'd leaned on Noah the other night. It was the first time she'd revealed that layer of herself to anyone. Not even Darrell had been witness to it. But then, they'd lived in the city, where those irrational fears didn't exist for her.

When she'd taken the children on the big hike, she'd been testing herself, and she had passed with flying colors. But that had been during the day. It was what she couldn't see that got to her— what was inside the darkness. She wanted so much for that fear to go away, to feel strong and capable in all aspects of her life.

"You aiming to catch the garter, too?" Noah asked, humor in his voice.

"What?"

He gestured to the small group of men encircling her as David knelt in front of Valerie to remove her garter.

Tricia forced a smile and left. Instead of returning to the table, she found her way to the back patio. She just needed some air.

Regrets, she thought again. She thought she'd banished them. She'd created her mantra as a way of eliminating regrets. And certainly she did believe that life was short, and she'd done a good job the past year of making it an adventure. So, why were regrets taking center stage again? Been there, done that. *Over* that. Or so she'd thought.

She inhaled her bouquet again. A little backsliding was probably realistic, especially at a wedding, where emotions ran a little higher.

"Tricia?" Noah's voice came soft in the darkness.

She moved into his line of sight. "I'm here."

"Are you okay?"

"I'm fine, thanks. Just needed a break."

"I'll leave you alone, then."

"Noah, wait. You don't need to go. The cool air feels good, doesn't it?"

He came up beside her. He'd taken off his jacket and tie long ago, and rolled up his shirt sleeves a few turns. He had in- credible arms, amazing hands. Watching him put his hands on one of his children always made her smile, and sometimes made her feel like weeping. Feeling his hands on her had a whole different response—and he'd barely touched her, aside from dancing.

"Who caught the garter?" she asked.

"David slung it at Joseph."

"Did it make a difference? Did Joseph go talk to Dixie?"

"I don't know. I came looking for you."

"Why?"

"To apologize for my behavior during the dance. You're right. I should've buried the issues with Jake long ago."

"So, will you now?"

He gave her an enigmatic look. "Maybe."

Tricia laughed. At least he was trying. He seemed to be doing a lot of trying lately—with his children, with her, with life in general. So, an old dog could learn new tricks, after all.

"Obviously, you're free to date whomever you want," he added.

"I appreciate that you're concerned," she said, grateful for his candor.

"Why did you take this job?" he asked, looking up, eyeing the stars that were out in full force. "Why did you even look for a job if you only had until January?"

"I like having a safety net, for one thing, but I also needed the money. Plus I have to keep busy."

"Won't you have enough from the sale of the house?"

"After my mother's savings ran out, we had to refinance the house a couple of times to cover her medical expenses, so there's not a whole lot of equity there. She had a small life insurance policy that financed my travels and should be enough for a down payment on a condo."

She wrapped her arms around herself, the chill of the night finally seeping through her dress into her skin. "I'd gone to Denise's agency hoping to get a job to tide me over, certainly never expecting she would have a position like yours. My understanding is that she mostly places clerical or domestic help. Lucky timing for me."

"And for my family," Noah said.

"You may want to reserve judgment on that."

He touched her shoulder. "You're cold. I wish I had my jacket to put around you."

"I won't stay out here much longer. Neither should you, since the kids are on their own."

"Gid's keeping an eye on them, but so will everyone else. It's a close community."

"I noticed." She shivered, but she didn't want to go back inside yet.

Without asking he put his arms around her and held her close to his body. "Warmer?"

"Yes, thanks."

Conversation stopped. She closed her eyes. Scent from the roses drifted from the bouquet she held behind him, adding to the emotion of the moment, reminding her of the wedding that never happened, the regrets that haunted her. Noah's hands were splayed over her back, twin spots of heat.

"Are weddings hard on you?" he asked close to her ear.

"They've always brought out the what-ifs. But then after my mother died, I vowed not to have regrets again, and I haven't. Not so far, anyway. But a few from the past still linger. Still have impact."

She didn't want to regret this moment with him, either, even though she knew it would change everything if she did what she wanted to do. The fact he'd taken her in his arms told her a whole lot. He wouldn't have done that for just anyone. He wanted to be close to her.

"How long do you think we have until someone comes looking for us?" she asked.

"Probably not much longer. Why?"

She'd never been the aggressor before. But then, she'd rarely wanted something as much as this. She would only regret it if she didn't try. "Because I need to do this."

She pulled his head down and kissed him, and after a moment of surprise, he kissed her back—no tender, explora-tory caress but a powerful action, his tongue seeking and finding, lips molding, breath mingling, hot and arousing. He groaned into her mouth, clasped her head with those big, beautiful hands and kissed her deeper than she remembered it was possible to do.

Tricia dropped her hands to his waist and pulled him even closer, feeling his need pressing into her. He slid a hand down her neck, dragged his fingertips along her heated skin then under the neckline of her dress. She sucked in a deep breath as he found her nipple, already aching for his touch.

"You're incredible," he whispered, his voice shaky, as he caressed her.

"So are you."

"We shouldn't—"

"Shh. No shouldn'ts. No regrets. No complications."

"I was going to say we shouldn't be standing right here where anyone can see." He moved her backward, out of sight of the door, and urged her against a post. "I've had dreams about you," he said, curving both hands over her breasts, thumbing both nipples, nipping at her mouth again and again.

"Same here." He felt wonderful. Exciting and arousing. Exotic and yet familiar somehow, too.

He took the kiss deep again, wedging a leg between hers, drawing his thigh up to press into her where she ached and throbbed. Not a single sound made it through the pleasure that had taken over her mind. She dug her fingers into his shirt and arched her back as his tongue made a hot, wet trail down her neck.

There! Don't stop. Please…

He stopped. Jerked back.

"Sorry," she heard someone say, then retreat, footsteps fading.

"Who was that?" she whispered, frantic.

"Gideon." Noah took a step back, looking around. He tucked his shirt in.

She hadn't realized she'd pulled it out.

"Regrets?" he asked.

"Well, yeah."

"I'm sorry, Tricia. I don't know why I let it get out of control. I know better."

She set her fingers on his lips. "I regret being interrupted."

He pulled her in for a last kiss. "I don't know what this means for us."

"I don't, either. We'll talk about it, I guess." She finger-combed her hair, then picked up the bouquet from where it had fallen on the ground. "I'll go first." Tricia went inside and slipped into the nearest restroom to put herself back together. She stared at her reflection and wondered if anyone else would see changes in her. She hadn't reached the ultimate point of satisfaction physically, and her hunger for it did more than linger now. She could see it in her own face, in the brightness of her eyes.

"Now what?" she asked aloud. The question echoed, in the room and in her head. She ran her fingers over her tender, well-kissed lips.

She wanted to finish what they started, to know what it felt like. What *he* felt like. No guessing. No wondering.

She didn't know how to make it happen. She only knew she wasn't done with him yet.

"I'm done," Noah said. "Won't happen again."

"Why don't I believe you?" Gideon asked. They were waiting outside the hotel for the limo coming to take David and Valerie to the airport for their honeymoon trip to Hawaii, the place she wanted most to see. "You told me the other night that you were going to keep your hands off her."

"She started it."

"What?"

"It's true. She kissed me first."

Gideon eyed him, making a point without words.

"I know," Noah said. "What can I say? I'm trying to verify the rumor that it is like riding a bicycle."

Gid laughed. "I guarantee you, you won't have forgotten how to do it."

"I know. You're right." Noah knew he'd made a mistake. He should've walked away once he found out she was okay. But he *had* forgotten how good it felt to kiss a woman. And caress her body. And taste her perfumed skin—especially *this* woman who'd been living in his house, driving him crazy just by existing.

"What are you going to do?" Gideon asked.

"Remember my priorities. I need her as the kids' teacher. I can't do anything to jeopardize that. They would never forgive me." Especially since he'd just seemed to finally start to connect again with them. He couldn't risk doing anything to ruin that. But he sure as hell wanted to strip Tricia naked and have his way with her just once.

"What's going on with your plan to start dating?" Gideon asked.

"I haven't asked anyone out yet, but I will. For Saturday night, when Tricia will be in Sacramento."

"Maybe it's best if she knows you're dating."

"I don't know if all the advice you're doling out so freely is all that great, Gid. You haven't exactly made the best choices in relationships yourself."

"Which is why you should pay attention to me. I've learned."

The limo pulled up, the Falcon Limited he'd taken the kids out in last weekend. On Monday it would be on its way to its new owner in Las Vegas. Noah directed the driver to a parking place they'd blocked off for him, then walked over with Gideon to make sure the champagne and food they'd ordered was in place.

"You know," Gid said thoughtfully, "maybe I'm all wrong

about this thing, this attraction. Maybe Tricia's someone you're thinking about marrying. You could have compromised your reputation and hers tonight if someone other than me had come across you, and, frankly, I've never known you to make that kind of misstep. You've always needed a complete picture of the outcome and consequences before you act."

Marrying? The idea was so far off Noah's radar, he barely paid attention to it. Noah knew exactly what was driving his irrational behavior. "Consider that I haven't had sex for three years, then rethink your comment."

Gid laughed. "Point taken."

"What about you? You spent most of the evening with Denise."

"She intrigues me."

Noah eyed him curiously.

"There's something about her," Gid said with a shrug. "Did you know she's blond?"

"Looks like a brunette to me."

"Nope. I find it curious that she dyes her hair brown. Do many blondes do that? I need to know why."

They went into the hotel to announce the limo had arrived. In the flurry of sending David and Valerie off, checking to make sure everyone who'd been drinking had a sober driver to take them home, and corralling the children, who were completely wound up from the punch and cake, Noah didn't even make eye contact with Tricia.

Finally they all climbed into the SUV for the drive home. She sat in the front seat beside him, her hands in her lap, a small smile on her face, looking sweet and innocent.

He liked that he knew she was a contradiction, that she could be sweet and did look innocent—if you didn't look below her neck—but he also knew how hot she was. How soft her lips were. How demanding her mouth was. How she wasn't afraid to be bold, to give as much as she gave.

Yeah, he was glad he knew that. And now that this new knowledge of her would be melding with his fantasies, his dreams would become more complex, more detailed.

What would happen next was anyone's guess.

Chapter Fourteen

Tricia stepped into her Sacramento house the next morning and was greeted with a sparkling fresh interior. Almost every surface had been painted or restained, giving her a fresh palette, and also a lot of work. She spent the morning moving furniture into place, trying different arrangements, but mostly trying to keep herself too busy to think.

No such luck.

She was bombarded with thoughts about Noah, had barely slept because of it. Need had arisen after a long period of dormancy. And in the light of day, she'd pretty much determined there was nothing she could do about it.

Even if they had wanted to risk taking things further last night with the kids in the house, Zach had complained of a stomachache, then had run to the bathroom and thrown up.

He didn't have a fever, so she guessed it was all the cake, mints, peanuts and other treats he'd overindulged in.

Tricia had been conflicted over what to do about him. Her instinct was to step in and take over, but it was past time that Noah learned to deal with a sick child instead of leaving it to the help.

Ultimately, Zach resolved the dilemma on his own when he asked Noah if he could sleep with him.

Noah had been so stunned that Tricia had almost laughed. He'd looked at her as if she would rescue him. She didn't accommodate him.

"Mom would've let me," Zach said, as Noah remained silent.

"Okay," Noah said, defeated by a nine-year-old's creative coercion. "Go get your pajamas on."

"Me, too," Adam said, his hand on his stomach. "I don't feel so good, either."

Tricia understood that the boys had never spent a night apart, so that on its own would've been hard for Adam. But factoring in the privilege of sleeping with Dad? Well, Adam could never allow himself to be trumped by Zach about that.

"Just keep an empty bucket handy," she'd said, patting the bewildered Noah on the arm as she went off to her own room, her body humming with anticipation that would find no satisfaction tonight—or maybe any night, once he had a chance to think it over.

"Deserter," he'd called to her as she reached her room, grinning.

Frustrated at not sleeping, Tricia had gotten up at four-thirty and headed for home, so she didn't know how Noah and the boys had done through the night.

She hated that she didn't know, but decided not to call and ask. Whatever she and Noah had to say to each other should be in person, not over the phone, where she couldn't see his expression or body language. Would he decide they'd made a mistake? Would he—rightly—blame her? He may have been an enthusiastic participant, but she'd definitely been the pursuer.

Oh, for heaven's sake. It was just a kiss. Why was she making such a big deal out of it, anyway? Just a kiss.

Right.

When the phone rang close to noon, she was headfirst into her refrigerator, giving it a good cleaning. She hoped it wasn't Noah. She needed space from him for one day, but she also needed to finish getting the house in order.

"Hi, Tricia."

She recognized the golden voice of Rudy Wiley, Realtor, and a dear and trusted friend of her mother. As a second career, he did voiceovers for local radio and television programs. He could make disasters seem okay with that smooth voice of his.

"Hey, Rudy. What's up?"

"I met a young couple at an open house yesterday. Told them about your house. They're interested."

Already? "But…it's not on the market yet. I'm not finished getting it ready."

"I explained that, and it doesn't matter to them. Can I bring them by today?"

She looked around her kitchen.

"Tricia." His voice soothed. "You know what the market's like. To have a buyer lined up before the For Sale sign goes up is almost unheard of."

She knew that. It was just that now it had become real. She would be leaving her childhood home, leaving the tangible memories of her parents, replacing them with only the visuals in her head, and photographs. She would be leaving her hometown for parts and people unknown.

"Okay," she said finally. "How about three o'clock?" She would have time to finish up and take a shower.

"Great. See you then."

She hung up, then sat on the floor and leaned against the door frame. Was she doing the right thing, selling the house, moving to San Diego? Starting over? She'd been so sure before.

Probably just seller's blues. She would get over it.

By the time Rudy and the couple showed up, everything looked shipshape. While they toured, she went outside and sat on the front porch swing, waving now and then at a neighbor. The neighborhood had undergone a change in the past few years, with several young families moving in, changing the landscape in that lots of children now played outdoors, and houses were now fixed up, looking fresh again. A new era. Revitalization. Cities depended on it for survival.

When the front door opened, she stood. The woman smiled and the man nodded, then they took off without a word. Tricia went inside to talk to Rudy. He passed her a sheet of paper.

"Here's their offer."

Tricia's eyes opened wide. "This is more than what you and I talked about for a starting point."

"I told them your asking price. They don't want it to go to market."

"But I thought this was a buyer's market."

"They love the house, Tricia. They want it. As is. You don't have to do anything else to it. There's a hitch, however."

She blew out the breath she realized she was holding. "Isn't there always?"

"They haven't qualified for a loan yet. In fact, they just decided yesterday to start looking. So, they'll put in loan apps tomorrow. You should hear sometime later in the week. It was part of their decision to offer you a little more, because they don't want you to entertain offers from someone else until they've got an answer on financing."

"Do you think it'll be an issue?"

"I don't know. It's a tight market for getting mortgages, too. So. What do you want to do? I've got a deposit check right here."

She liked the idea that a young couple just starting out would be living in her house, maybe even have their first baby there, bring new life to it. "I'm game."

"They'd want a thirty-day escrow. Would that be a problem?"

"I have a place to stay," she said, considering it, knowing for sure she could stay with Noah and the kids. But maybe she could ask a friend if she could spend weekends in Sacramento. Or perhaps Denise. They had something in common now—Falcon men. At least Denise had a chance for a normal relationship.

"All right then, thanks," Rudy said. "I'll be in touch. You did a great job fixing up the place. Your mom would've been pleased."

She hugged him, happy to be with someone who remembered her mother, and who also reminded her that she was making the right decisions for herself. She just needed to stay on track, follow her dream, reach the goal. It was all there, within reach.

An hour later she pulled into Noah's garage. The SUV was gone. Her mind swam with possibilities. Zach had gotten sicker. Or it'd been his appendix, not overindulgence. Or one of them had gotten hurt. Adam caught another animal and it'd bit him. They were all at the hospital.

She pulled out her cell phone just as the big black Caddy turned into the driveway. All the kids except Zoe waved at her. Everyone looked to be safe and sound.

"Miss Tricia! Miss Tricia!" Zach shouted as soon as the car door opened. "We went to the Railroad Museum in Old Sacramento. It was awesome. We could go inside the trains and everything. They were humongous."

The children all piled out. Zoe headed toward the house without saying hello. Adam waved and took off after her. Ashley and Zach brought up the rear. Tricia looked at Noah. He looked back in a way she couldn't describe but could feel.

"How was your day?" he asked as they all trooped up to the house.

Her roaming thoughts were jarred back into the moment. "It

was fine. I got a lot of work done." She decided not to tell him about the offer until the sale went through. *If* it went through. "Sounds like you all had fun."

"I think everyone enjoyed it. I know Ashley liked the restaurant where we ate lunch. And they all went a little wild in one of the candy stores."

He was driving her crazy. No hints at all about how he felt? No, "we'll talk later," or something like that? Just keep her on pins and needles, instead?

"How was your sleepover?" she asked.

"Not a whole lot of sleep involved. Adam and Zach are huge bed hogs."

"Used to having their beds to themselves," she said.

"As am I."

"Me, too." An image of them sleeping together blinked once then disappeared. "What's in the grocery bag?"

He hefted it. "Dinner. All the fixings for ice cream sundaes. We had a really healthy lunch," he added as reasoning.

He was different today. Looser, livelier. Why?

"Something wrong with Zoe?" she asked.

"Apparently, but I don't know what. She was sulking all day."

Adam stuck his head out the back door. "Dad! Miss Tricia! Come watch the movie."

"I made the mistake of leaving him in charge of the video camera," Noah said. "I apologize in advance for what's bound to make us all seasick to watch."

She was just happy that they'd done something as a family, something she hadn't even recommended or urged them to.

And she also felt a little left out. She wanted her cake and to eat it, too.

After she tucked the children into bed, Tricia headed for Noah's office. She hadn't rehearsed what to say to him. She figured it would just evolve, based on what he had to say. But when she got there, he was on the phone.

"Overseas," he whispered, covering the mouthpiece. "I'll be a while."

Tricia didn't go back to her room but grabbed a jacket from the utility room peg, went outdoors and sat on the stairs, close enough for a quick retreat into the house, if necessary, but needing to face her fears, needing to feel strong about something.

Because she was weak about Noah. Now that they'd kissed, she felt different. Kind of irresistible, even. Would it lead to more? Should it? She wasn't going to be there forever. Would it be so bad if they gave in to the attraction. Who could it hurt?

She wondered which scenario had the potential for the most regrets—sleeping with him, then moving on, or not sleeping with him, then moving on? Which could cause the most regrets for *him?*

Did it matter? If the point was not to have regrets at all, she needed an option three. What could that possibly be?

Tricia jumped as something emerged from the trees. She hunched, making herself small, then realized it was Bear. Was he friendly? He'd hightailed it away the other night, happy to be free of his trap, and Noah said Bear didn't like people.

"Bear," she called softly. He went perfectly still, looked her way. "C'mere, boy."

He came cautiously, stopping a few feet away and sniffing the air. He inched closer. She waited, not moving. "Hey, boy. How are you?"

He raised his muzzle, as if answering.

"Do you like your ears scratched? C'mere."

He got within a few inches, then took a quick step back when she reached to touch him. "It's okay. I'm a friend."

He closed the gap, setting his head on her knees. She rubbed him gently, his fur long and soft. After a few seconds he whipped around and took off, probably hearing something outside her range.

Yes, she was definitely going to get a dog after she got situated in San Diego. Someone to talk to, a buddy to go for walks with, to pet while they watched television on the sofa together. He'd have a great dog name and be so well behaved that everyone would welcome him into their homes. She wouldn't be alone.

Tricia made herself walk down the driveway to the end of the house. She hovered there, straining to peer into the darkness. She'd seen wet paw prints across the deck a few times. Noah identified them as a raccoon once, then a fox. She didn't want to encounter either one, even with assurances that they were more afraid of her than she of them.

She made herself stand there until she counted to sixty, then hurried back to the house, making as little noise as possible. As she headed toward his office, she saw the office door was closed, a sliver of light indicating he was inside.

Closed? So, he didn't want to talk to her? Was that what that meant?

An image of throwing open his office door, barging in, swiping his desktop clean with her arm and having her way with him grabbed hold and wouldn't shake loose. Maybe the option three she was looking for was just to do it and then worry about it later.

It was so unlike her. She liked being safe, even as she searched for adventure. She didn't have much practice in being a femme fatale. Would he notice? Would he care?

What are you doing? He's your boss.

The loud voice in her head would talk her out of it, if she let it, so she gave it an equally loud answer: *Trying not to have regrets. You know he won't make a move unless he knows it's what you want, too. Maybe not even then.*

She waited. No other sound came to her. No pro and con list. No admonitions of any kind.

Should she dare? Could she pull it off?

Tricia put her shoulders back and knocked on his door.

"Come in."

She did, shutting the door behind him. He sat back, eyeing her with interest.

"I thought we should talk," she said.

"About what?"

"Last night." Gathering every bit of nerve she owned, she moseyed around to his side of the desk then leaned against it, bracing herself with her hands behind her. Could she sweep his desk clean in one swoop or just end up looking like an idiot? She picked up a letter opener and toyed with it, enjoying the way he watched her, his brows raised. She was showing him a new Tricia McBride, one completely out of character. She figured he was as shocked by that as she was.

He plucked the letter opener from her before she poked a hole in the paper she was twirling it into. "You're cold." He took her hand between his to warm it, then gathered the other one, too.

"I've been outdoors for a while."

"Really? Why?"

"Facing fears."

"Good for you."

"I didn't go far. Bear came to visit, though. He was friendly."

After a few beats, he said, "You wanted to talk about last night?"

It's time, she decided. *You're not going to be here forever. Go ahead. Take a chance. No regrets.*

Fly without your safety net....

Noah waited, fascinated. She looked both nervous and, well, sexy.

"Is everything okay between us now?" she asked. "You said last night that you didn't know what it meant for us. The kiss," she added, as if he didn't remember.

He remembered—how she tasted, how she felt. "It's been on my mind."

"Does it change anything?"

His stomach tightened at the possibilities. "That's a loaded question. I'm male. I'm human. I want. But…"

"But I'm your employee."

"In part."

"Short-term employee," she said, looking unsure suddenly.

"Why does that make a difference?" He wasn't being as honest as she was. He knew he was trying to get her to stay. She didn't know that.

Silence rang in the room. "Okay, then," she said finally, as if it didn't matter. "Good night." She left the room.

Noah leaned back and shut his eyes. He'd convinced himself the kiss had been an anomaly last night. He thought she felt the same. And he needed to keep on track—his children needed her to stay. So did *he*. He had to convince her this job was more important than her other one.

What now?

According to Gideon, there was only one way to get Tricia off his mind, to deflect his attraction, and that was to start dating. On the other hand, he'd promised his children there would be no more changes.

He had to think this through, as he would a business problem.

Okay. Option one: Give up on the possibility of keeping her and hire someone else, taking the time he needed to find exactly the right person.

Option two: Ignore his attraction to her and try and get her to stay.

Option three: Was there one? The only thing left was to marry her.

The consequences of option one meant he could sleep with her, since she would be leaving. He liked that possibility, except it had an end date attached to it, and it meant his children would lose her.

Consequences of option two meant not sleeping with her, but his household would run smoothly, and his children would be loved and cared for and taught well, which would make his life easier. Easier for what? He couldn't answer that yet. He'd just come out of a black pit that had lasted three years. He didn't know what would happen next.

And the consequences of option three meant he'd be married. Good consequence in terms of sleeping with her and his children being happy, but long term? They hadn't known each other long, hadn't fallen in love, making option three only a back-burner possibility down the road.

His goal was to keep his children happy. They were connecting again, laughing together, playing together. He needed that to continue, and Tricia was a key element in that happening. So. Option number two: He would need to ignore his attraction and get her to stay, even if that was the hardest personal choice.

Noah shoved his hands through his hair. He hadn't asked a woman out in about fourteen years, but the process couldn't have changed much. He flipped through his Rolodex, located the phone number he wanted, then dialed.

"Hello?"

"Cynthia, it's Noah. I hope it's not too late to call."

"Not at all. Is everything okay?"

"Yes, fine, thanks." He plowed on, no small talk, no building up to it. "I was wondering if you'd like to go to dinner with me on Saturday night."

A stretch of silence followed. Obviously he'd really caught her off guard.

"Would it be too awkward, since you work with my children? I understand if that would be an issue for you."

"No, I— Noah, I'd love to go to dinner with you."

"Great. I'll pick you up around seven?"

"Sure. Okay."

"See you then." He hung up. He was moving forward.

A moment later Tricia appeared in his doorway again. Had she overheard? He waited for her to speak first.

"I'm sorry," she said, taking a few tentative steps in. "I just need to clarify that we are just going on as if nothing happened, right? I know it was just a kiss, but it mattered to me."

His options and consequences ran through his head again. When he said nothing in return, she headed out the door.

"Sorry I bothered you. I won't again, I assure you."

He watched her disappear around the corner. Option two flew out the door behind her, disappearing, vetoed by the consequences of option one: He could sleep with her.

He didn't wait a second more but raced from the room to catch up with her. He beat her to the staircase, put himself in front of her.

"You are one tempting woman," he said, the words dragging along his throat. Then he kissed her, not tenderly, not teasingly, but as a man with a fierce desire, no matter how many reasons he had for not acting on it.

"Are you sure?" he asked, his voice gruff.

"Yes. Oh, yes."

It was enough permission for him. This was human need after a three-year drought with a consenting adult who wanted him, too.

Noah slid his hands down to her thighs, picked her up and carried her back to his office, her legs wrapped around him, their mouths still fused. She was a whole armful of woman, all curves and temptation. Deep, arousing sounds transferred from her mouth to his, vibrating down his throat.

He locked the door behind them, then lowered her to the

couch, moving back only long enough to pull his shirt over his head and toss it aside. His jaw felt locked, his skin hot, his breath hard to catch, especially when she touched his chest, dragging her fingertips from his collarbone to his waist, lingering there.

He needed to be skin to skin with her. He peeled her sweater over her head, tossing it toward his. She sat up as he reached behind her to unhook her bra, sliding it off her, then he cradled her breasts with his hands. Her amazing breasts.

"So, you thought about me today?" he asked, his hands in constant motion, his fingers stroking her nipples. He dragged his lips along her jaw, then moved low to take a nipple into his mouth. Ah the glorious feel of her puckered skin, surrounded by smooth, firm flesh. The stuff of dreams.

She arched up. Goose bumps rose on her skin as his tongue made a trail then retraced it, over curves, into valleys, onto peaks.

"I thought about you *some* of the time," she finally answered, her breath catching as he tugged lightly at a nipple with his teeth, not wanting to rush so much, but knowing he couldn't hold out for long.

"You're not very flattering." She felt incredible to him. Perfect. Everything he'd thought she would be, and more.

"You have a big enough ego," she said, a smile in her voice.

She moaned as he cupped her between her legs, rotating his thumb, pleased at her reaction. All sense of playfulness stopped. She writhed beneath his touch, giving herself up to what he offered.

The couch was small for two people so tall. He considered taking her upstairs to his bedroom, but he figured that might give them both too much time to think about the consequences....

Consequences be damned. She wanted it as much as he did. He wasn't taking advantage. There would be equal satisfaction, and equal blame, if it came to that.

He slipped to his knees alongside the sofa, giving himself

space to undress her the rest of the way. She was having as much trouble breathing as he was. Anywhere he touched her he could feel her pulse pounding.

"I wonder whose heart is beating faster?" he said, laying his hand over her heart.

"Mine. Definitely mine. And I'm going to explode if you don't keep things moving along."

He laughed, soft and low, at her demands. "Yes, ma'am."

The snap of her jeans popped open easily. He kissed the skin revealed, moving down as he pulled on the zipper, his head filling with her heat and her scent. She lifted her hips as he tugged at her jeans.

"You're on the pill, right?" he asked, some amount of sense surfacing for a moment.

"The pill? What— Oh." She let her hips drop. "No."

He sat back on his heels slowly. His chest heaved. He dragged a hand over his mouth, forced himself to meet her gaze, seeing confusion there. Well, this created a big problem, because he didn't have any condoms. Hadn't needed any.

"Um, maybe this would be a good time to tell you something else," she said, sitting up, using her arms to partly cover her breasts. "I, uh, this is the first, uh— I'm a virgin."

For a long moment he couldn't say anything. Think anything.

"Say something," she said.

"You can't be."

Her eyes went wide. "Your disbelief doesn't change the fact that I am."

"I'm sorry. I—I don't know what to say." And he didn't. He was just…shocked. "This changes things."

"Why?" She looked bewildered.

He ran his hand down her hair, wanting to soothe. She pulled back, clearly hurt.

"This isn't the way to lose your virginity, Tricia. On a couch, in my office? It's not right." He picked up her bra and sweater and passed them to her, then he grabbed up his shirt, turning away, giving her privacy to dress, talking so that she would be less uncomfortable, as if anything could erase the discomfort of the moment. "You don't have birth control. I don't have birth control. More than one reason to stop."

"I'm dressed. You can turn around now." Her voice sounded strong and sure, not embarrassed. She sat primly, her hands locked in her lap, her eyes vacant. "I agree we didn't really think this through. I mean, the whole birth control business. You'll have to forgive me, since I don't have a lot of experience at this sort of thing. It was kind of a spur-of-the-moment, heat-of-the-moment thing."

What did one say at a time like this? He had no idea, didn't even want to continue the conversation, although he was curious how she could make it to age thirty-four and still be a virgin.

"I apologize, Tricia. I seem to lose control when I'm with you," he said, telling her more than he probably should, but not wanting her to be hurt too much.

"I'm sorry, too, Noah. But you don't need to worry. I won't let it happen again. Back to business for both of us." She smiled in a way that said she was confident and okay, then it faltered a bit, just enough to know she was hurt, and nothing he could say or do would change that. Only time would.

"That would be for the best," he said. "Business."

She walked out the door, shutting it with a quiet click behind her.

He sat behind his desk, not even sure where to begin focusing his thoughts. He hated that she'd been hurt, but it was impossible to take steps back, to alter time. They had to live with it.

And he had to make sure it stayed that way. His children needed her.

But now, recalling the look in her eyes as she'd left the room, he wondered if it wasn't too late. They'd crossed a bridge that had blown up behind them, leaving them no choice but to find another path.

Chapter Fifteen

Tricia stood with Joseph on the back deck, supervising the children as they raked the tilled ground. The putting-green sod would be installed in a few days, much to Zach's delight.

A few days had passed since her disastrous encounter with Noah in his office. She hadn't let herself cry about it. They'd agreed. Business only. It was a good decision, she kept reminding herself, but she wanted to be sure the kids didn't pick up on any tension, so she went out of her way to be friendly with him. He seemed to be doing the same in return—when he was home. He hadn't come home in time for dinner Monday and Tuesday, had barely made it in time for their individual meetings in his office. Her own meetings in his office were brief. He stayed behind his desk, keeping the division between them.

Without him at the dinner table, tension hung in the air as the children stared at his empty chair now and then, even though conversation continued, something they'd gotten good at, whether or not Noah was there.

Was he avoiding her? If so, he needed to stop, because the kids were being hurt by it.

"Jake asked about you," Joseph said, leaning on the railing, giving Tricia a quick look. "He said that *you* said he could call."

She'd completely forgotten that, not exactly a compliment to Jake. "I did say that."

"So, I should give him your cell number?"

Should he? Would dating someone else help? "All you McCoy men are interesting, Joseph."

"I hear a *but* coming."

"*But,* I'm at a point in life where I'm looking to settle down, and I hear you all have a problem with commitment."

He straightened, crossed his arms. "I don't need another speech about Dixie."

"I don't plan on giving one." Although she wished she could say something that would make him act. Dixie was miserable without him. It didn't take a psychic to see that.

She stopped the thought from going further. Obviously she'd gotten in too deep already with this community if she was overly concerned with whether two people she barely knew would reconcile. "I'm just telling you, Joseph, that I'm done with dating for the sake of dating. I want a home and family."

"What makes you think Jake doesn't want the same thing? Why not give him a shot?"

She was human enough to consider that dating Jake might prompt a little jealousy from Noah, but to what purpose? What would it change? And what an adolescent idea, anyway.

"Miss Tricia?"

Startled, Tricia turned around. Ashley offered up two glasses of iced tea. She'd gotten good at avoiding the dirtier work in the yard, plus she'd suddenly started hovering around Tricia now that her father wasn't home much.

"You both looked thirsty," Ashley said, her smile irresistible, as always.

"Thank you." Tricia took a sip. Ashley had said she'd left her gloves in the utility room, then had stalled a good ten minutes before coming back. "Did you find your gloves?"

She pulled them from her pocket. "I think I should just supervise today. I'm getting a blister."

"Let me see," Joseph said.

She stuck out her hand. He examined it closely. "Where? Here? This tiny spot?"

She looked herself then nodded.

"No sweat," Joseph said dismissively. "Best thing for it? Hold that finger away from the rake. Don't let it have contact."

It wasn't the answer Ashley wanted. With a little toss of her head, she tugged on the gloves and joined her siblings as a van came down the driveway. Cynthia Madras climbed out and headed over. Something was different about her, Tricia thought, not putting her finger on what it was, except for the fact she looked friendlier than the first time they met.

"I'm sorry it took so long for me to bring your supplies," she said, climbing onto the deck. "Several items were on back order."

"Can I get anything out of your van for you?" Joseph asked.

"Would you? That would be great, thanks. The three boxes behind the driver's seat. If you could just put them inside the house, please? Tricia and I don't need to go through them. They're self-explanatory." She came up to the railing as Joseph left. "Hi, kids!"

They acknowledged her with waves. Ashley said she'd get Cynthia a glass of iced tea and hurried off.

"Busy bees," she commented to Tricia, after they'd stood and watched for a while.

"They're having a good time, I think. Even Zach, who's not big on being outdoors, and Ashley, who's 'really not into manual labor,' as she puts it." Tricia smiled at the memory of Ashley making that announcement. "It's been a good project for them as a family."

Adam took that moment to hurl a dirt clod at Zoe's feet, splattering it over her shoes. She retaliated, and a war began.

"Aren't you going to stop them?" Cynthia asked.

Tricia heard the disapproval in her voice. "Not unless they start hurting each other. They're just having fun."

"I wonder if Noah would approve."

Killjoy. Tricia decided it was a good thing that Cynthia supervised, not taught. What a dull classroom that would be.

"I think Noah likes what I'm doing with his children," Tricia said. "I'm sure he'd tell me if he wasn't happy."

"I've known Noah a *lot* longer than you, and I can tell that he keeps quite a bit to himself. Tell you what, I'll see what I can find out at dinner Saturday night, then let you know."

Tricia felt swept in a tornado that swirled her violently around and around. Dinner? Saturday? He had a *date?*

All she could do was look at Cynthia. Words stuck in her throat, where her heart had lodged. Her mind was busy, however. *Well, you idiot. Business only. What'd you expect?*

"Can you keep a secret?" Cynthia asked, unaware of the emotions warring inside Tricia.

After a moment, Tricia nodded. When had he made the date? After their disastrous encounter? Before? Which was worse?

"If Jessica had told me she was quitting, I would've given up my job to be their teacher. I would've done anything to get Noah to notice me. As a woman, I mean. But now you're here, and he seems much more relaxed, much less worried about things in general, and he finally asked me out. So, thank you."

The tornado dropped Tricia back on the ground, feet first, hard. She wanted to wipe that gloating smile off Cynthia's face. That was what was different about her today. She looked…smug.

"Miss Cynthia?" Ashley said from behind them. "Here's your tea."

"Thank you, sweetie."

"You're welcome." Without being ordered to, she went back to work, Joseph having intervened in the dirt fight as it had escalated.

Tricia continued to say nothing to Cynthia, who rattled on in a gratingly endless monologue, like fingernails on a chalkboard.

"You don't come across a lot of men like Noah," Cynthia said with a sigh. "You know, financially secure, someone you wouldn't have to worry about straying."

And he's kind, Tricia thought. Well intentioned. A loving father who was getting better at it all the time. Handsome. Sexy…

Tricia spent the rest of the day brooding. Then Noah made the mistake of coming home late again, long after dinner.

She didn't even try to be friendly this time, but went to her room and stayed there until Ashley knocked, telling her they were ready for bed.

"Are you okay?" Ashley asked as they walked to her room.

Tricia put her arm around the girl's shoulders. "I'm a little tired today. Nothing to be worried about."

"Are you mad at Dad?"

Obviously she needed to maintain better control of her emotions in front of the kids. "Why do you think that?"

"Because he's been late every night, which means you have to hang out with us longer."

"Oh, honey. That's not it at all. I love being with you." She hugged Ashley a little tighter.

"But we wear you out."

Tricia laughed. "Sometimes, yes, but in a good way. You bring me a whole lot of joy."

"We like you, too."

Tricia knew that was true of Ashley, Adam and Zach. As for Zoe? Tricia wasn't too sure. She seemed to get more distant, more…surly, every day, the only one who hadn't warmed up to her.

On the other hand, Zoe wasn't treating Noah any better.

After Tricia told them all good-night, she went downstairs to Noah's office. He looked up from his paperwork when she knocked on his open door. She shut the door before she took a seat across the desk from him.

"Do we have a problem?" he asked.

"You are undoing everything good that's happened in the past few weeks. Everything."

He leaned back. "In what way?"

"You know exactly."

"Probably, but why don't you tell me, in case I'm missing anything."

"Don't be condescending."

He put down his pen and dragged a hand down his face. "I apologize. You're right. I'm making you pay for my mistakes. Please. Go ahead and tell me what's wrong."

"First of all, Noah, we both made a mistake. Equal blame, okay? But more importantly, you need to be home for dinner. They've come to count on it. It hurts their feelings, especially since you haven't explained why. What *is* the reason, anyway?"

"It's work related."

She didn't believe him. "Work *created*, it looks to me. You're avoiding me, for the obvious reasons, I think, but the upshot is that it's hurting the children."

He was quiet for a while. "Again, you're right. I was avoiding you. I lost control the other night. I don't lose control. Ever. I didn't know how to handle it."

"The same way I'm handling it. By forgetting it happened." Which was so far from the truth, it was pitiful. It was all she thought about—how it had felt to be in his arms, to kiss and be kissed, to touch and be touched. To be desired. "Now. Change of subject. What can I do to help you find my replacement?"

His expression never changed. "I'm taking care of it."

"Fine. If that's all?" She started to stand.

"No. Please." He gestured for her to sit. "In all that's happened, I haven't asked you about the job you've taken. I'd like to know what makes it your dream job."

She set her hands in her lap. "It's as director of curriculum for a chain of private girls' schools, grades kindergarten through eighth. The corporate office is in San Diego. They have twelve locations in the western U.S."

"What qualifies you?"

"While I was taking care of my mom, I got my master's with a concentration in curriculum. I've always been interested in *what* we teach, how it affects overall education."

"But you don't have actual work experience in the field?"

"No."

He frowned.

"I know, I know," she said. "How'd I get the job without experience?"

"Can't help but wonder."

"My closest friend from college holds the position now. She's pregnant and wants to take off a year, maybe longer, to spend with her baby. She also doesn't want to lose her job. So she convinced the board to take me on in the interim."

He sat up straighter. "You mean the job is temporary?"

"Yes. But a very good addition to my resume."

"You're going to sell your house, pull up roots altogether, for a temporary job?"

What good had roots done her? she thought. "Lots of people do that for their careers."

"I never would have pegged you as being that career oriented."

She opened her mouth to argue his chauvinistic point.

He put up a hand. "No need to get huffy, Tricia. Obviously you're an exceptional teacher, but I just don't see you as someone who would ever put career above family."

"The only immediate family I have is a grandfather who's living it up in retirement with his new young wife." He'd struck a deep nerve, though. She wouldn't have anyone special to care for when she left his employ, and it was fine with her. Just fine. She'd done her share.

"On the subject of family," he said, after some time passed. "I got a call from the children's grandparents today. They usually have the kids for Thanksgiving week, but they need to bump it up. My mother-in-law is going to have foot surgery. She wants the kids while she's still mobile."

"So, what's the plan?"

"I'll drive them to San Luis Obispo on Sunday."

"Will you stay over?"

"No. I need to be in the office on Monday."

"That's a long drive in one day, there and back."

"Can't be helped."

"I guess you'd better not stay out too late with Cynthia Saturday night, then, hmm?" she said with a bright smile. "Do you have a sitter lined up?"

His jaw turned to marble. "Not yet."

"I'll stay here, then. Since they're leaving on Sunday and I won't see them for a week, I'd like to stay until you all take off."

A beat passed. "Okay. Thanks."

"You're welcome," she said with forced lightness. "Are we done?"

His mouth tightened. "Looks like it."

"You'll be here for dinner tomorrow night?"

"Yes."

"Thank you. Good night." Her knees were shaking as she left. She shouldn't have done that, shouldn't have mentioned the date. Big mistake. Bad move. Her jealousy was obvious.

She got to her bedroom and sat on the bed. What now? He'd apparently made a clean break of his attraction to her and was moving on.

She should do the same. In fact, she could call Joseph's brother, Jake, and line up a date. She didn't know why she'd told Joseph she wasn't looking to date for the sake of dating anymore. She was temporary. Jake would be temporary. So, why not? No chance to become dependent on him and have him go away, like everyone else.

Like everyone else?

Tricia moved to look out the window. "Since when have you become so cynical?" she asked aloud. There was a big difference between someone dying and someone leaving.

"But the end result's the same," she said, her breath fogging the window a little. She dragged a finger through it, then realized she'd drawn a heart with a crack down the middle.

Noah retreated to his bedroom, even though it was only nine o'clock. He flipped on the television, stretched out on his bed with the remote, channel surfed, then left it on a Kings' game, catching the score before tuning it out. He just needed background noise. Too much quiet resulted in too much thinking.

But thoughts intruded anyway. He'd actually forgotten about the date he'd made with Cynthia. He didn't have to look too far as to why it had slipped his mind. Nor did he have to look too far for an answer to the question of how Tricia found out about his date. Ashley told him Cynthia had stopped by earlier.

He didn't know why he'd expected her to stay quiet about it. Why should she? And in a small town like Chance City, news would travel.

Now that Tricia knew, it would hover between them, an issue that was personal, not open to discussion.

He was surprised she'd brought it up. But then she'd never been a normal employee, had rarely deferred to him. The way she'd spoken to him about being home to have dinner with the kids? No one else would've dared to tell how to run his life.

Even Margie, he thought. She'd been stubborn at times, but she was very traditional, especially about roles and the division of labor. He'd been the head of the household. After a mutual discussion, she would've let him make what decision needed making. She never would've told him what to do.

You like Tricia because she does tell you, he admitted to himself.

His life with Margie had been good, very good, with few bumps in the road. Maybe a tiny bit of resentment on her part now and then for them never doing anything out of the ordinary, for the way he'd always wanted to just stay home with her and the kids. The resentment cropped up every once in a while then would go away.

His business was much more stable now. If she'd lived, their lives would've been different.

Well, maybe not. Maybe they'd been too entrenched in routine for many changes to be made. Tricia had forced changes.

After another minute Noah left his room, walked to the opposite end of the hall and knocked on her door. He could hear the television on, then the sound stopped. She opened the door. She hadn't changed into whatever she wore to bed.

She didn't say a word, but he saw worry in her eyes while she waited for him to speak.

"I just want to tell you thank you."

Her brows drew together. "For what?"

"For everything you've done for us. All of us. No one else has had anywhere near the impact as you. We all appreciate it."

She swallowed. Her voice got soft. "Thank you."

He nodded then started to turn away.

"Noah?"

"Yes?"

"I think it's good you're dating. And Cynthia is very nice."

Nice. He'd had that once before with Margie, and it was good. Fine. But Tricia's more in-your-face approach left him…energized. Involved.

"Good night, Noah."

She closed the door slowly, as if giving him an opportunity to say something. Then when it was shut tight it seemed like she'd just closed an even bigger, heavier door between them, one that locked from the inside, leaving him no way to get in, even if he wanted to.

Chapter Sixteen

Noah was true to his word, coming home for dinner the rest of the week, spending time with them. He and Tricia never talked about his date again. Not one word. They'd lost their communication skills together, asking and answering questions but nothing more. Small talk.

On Saturday they all went to Zoe's last soccer game for the year, then to a pizza party with the whole team for a presentation of awards.

Tricia thought Noah would burst his buttons when Zoe was given a trophy for most goals scored and a special award voted by her teammates as the most helpful player.

Tricia had never seen Zoe so happy. All the little girls gathered around her, squealing and laughing, hugging her. Tricia didn't know *that* Zoe at all. How could she be so different away from home?

"We need to talk about Zoe," Tricia said to Noah when they

arrived home, keeping him back by the car while the kids went ahead. He'd told her he would be leaving the house at six-forty-five. She had two hours to get through, two hours to keep up the appearance that she wasn't dying inside at the thought of him holding another woman's hand, kissing her, embracing her.

"What about Zoe?" he asked.

"About what's wrong with her."

He looked baffled. "I don't know what you mean."

"You haven't noticed how withdrawn she's become? How little she's actually eating? Except for at the pizza parlor, when was the last time you saw her smile?"

"She's always been serious."

"Noah, this isn't her being serious. She's got a problem. It's eating away at her."

"Did you ask her about it?"

"We had a one-sided conversation this morning. I let her know she could come to me anytime, tell me anything. She said okay and off she went."

"I'll talk to her."

"Good. While you do that, I think I'll go for a drive." She didn't need to hang around the house, waiting for him to go. "I'll be back before you leave. Since they just had pizza, I know they'll be okay to eat dinner a little later. Cora left plenty of spaghetti for me to reheat. See you in a bit," she said, not giving him options. She got in her car and left, watching in her rearview mirror as he walked up the driveway.

She didn't know where to go. Valerie was still on her honeymoon. She liked Dixie but didn't know her well enough to just drop in. Denise lived in Sacramento, so no time to make a connection there.

Tricia had gotten used to being alone. Her mother hadn't been very communicative during the last year of her life, and Tricia had been mostly alone since then. Oh, she'd talked to a lot of people, but it wasn't the same as having someone along for the ride, someone to share a gorgeous sunrise or sunset, or even a meal, except at diner counters in various towns across the country. The healing process had necessitated her finding out who she was at that point in her life.

But now? Now she'd been living with five people, had gotten used to the noise and activity, and the fact that someone was always around to talk to, or laugh with, or share a meal. She'd put down roots already, although not deeply set ones, just tentacles dipping into the surface soil of their community.

When she moved, those roots would be pulled up, and new seeds planted in San Diego, only to be torn up again and tossed away when she had to leave that job. Wasn't there a good compromise between independence and deep roots?

Tricia drove into the tiny downtown, deciding to window-shop. As she wandered, people waved and nodded. She didn't know any of them, but she smiled and was happy to be acknowledged.

"Tricia?" Jake McCoy came up beside her. "Hi. Doing a little shopping?"

"Killing time," she answered.

"Me, too. Want to kill it together at the Lode? Can I buy you a cup of coffee?"

She pictured Noah and Cynthia at dinner, gazing at each other over candlelight. "Thank you. I'd like that."

He took her arm as they crossed the street. She glanced at her watch.

"Do you have an appointment?"

"I need to get back to the house by six-thirty."

"Tell you what. I'll keep an eye on the time, if you'll just sit back and relax."

She smiled, appreciating his desire to spend time with her. "You've got yourself a deal."

They'd no sooner taken seats in the diner when her cell

phone rang. She saw it was Rudy, her Realtor, and went outside to take the call.

"You're in the money," he said. "They got the loan."

"That's…great," she said, finding it hard to breathe.

"Tricia?"

"What?"

"Everything's going to be fine. It's a big change, but it'll be good. Your mother would be so proud of you." He talked more about the deal and paperwork and closing, but she heard little of it. "I think maybe we should talk tomorrow or Monday," he said.

"That would be better. Bye, Rudy. Thanks."

"Everything okay?" Jake asked, coming up beside her.

She couldn't get a word out. She looked at him, helpless, devastated, feeling like her memory had been wiped free of her history, good and bad. She didn't want to start over. She didn't want to give up her house, her roots. What had she done?

Tears spilled down her cheeks.

Her car. She needed to get to her car. She ran up the street. Just as she reached her goal, Jake caught up with her, turned her to face him, then pulled her into his arms and held her tight.

He didn't ask any questions. She told him nothing. She just wanted to go home.

And now she had no home.

Noah paced. If Tricia wasn't home in five minutes he would be late to Cynthia's, but more than his being late, he was bothered by the fact that Tricia was. She was a responsible person. If she could have called, she would have.

The phone rang. His "Hello" sounded harsh even to him.

"What's going on?" Gideon said. "What's wrong?"

Noah shoved his fingers through his hair. "Nothing. I don't know. Maybe something. Tricia was supposed to be here by now or I'm going to be late—" He spotted her car headed down the driveway. Relief and anger dueled in his mind, neither and both coming up the winner. "Here she is."

"Where are you headed?"

"Dinner date with Cynthia. I don't have time to talk, Gid."

"All right. All right. I'd been wondering if you'd worked up the nerve to ask her out, then I spotted Tricia and Jake hugging downtown today. Figured you'd backed away from her. That's good, Noah."

What? Tricia and Jake? *What?* How long had that been going on?

"I gotta go." He hung up the phone as Tricia rushed in.

"I'm so sorry, Noah. I'm never late—"

He grabbed her by the arms, holding her still, staring at her. "What's wrong? What happened?"

"Nothing. I—"

"You've been crying."

"It's nothing. Really. I'm fine." She wriggled free. "You need to go."

He studied her for another long moment. She was panting from running up the driveway. She looked nothing like her normal self. He would push harder later for some answers, not only to why she'd been crying, but what it had to do with Jake.

He made a quick trip into the family room to say goodbye. The boys waved. The girls barely acknowledged him. He'd hoped he would have a couple more years before they took on the rite of passage called adolescent unpredictability. No such luck.

"Did you talk to Zoe?" Tricia asked as he headed out the door.

"Yeah. I couldn't get anything out of her, either. I'm clueless."

She smiled. "Well, I could've told you that."

He was glad to see her smile, glad to have her joke with him, although it didn't change the fact she *had* been crying. She didn't seem like a woman who cried easily.

"Go. Have fun," she said.

He took his time walking to his car and backing out. The night was beautiful, crystal clear. When he hit the open road, he stayed at the speed limit, not in a hurry for what was ahead.

He pulled up in front of Cynthia's house, rang her bell. She opened the door, smiling, looking very nice, all dressed up.

Nice. There was that word again.

"Hello, Noah. Would you like to come in for a few minutes first? I don't know when our reservations are, but, if there's time…?"

He stepped inside and shut the door. Before she could lead the way, he stopped her. "I'm sorry, Cynthia. I can't do this. I came to tell you and to apologize. I realized I'm just not ready to date."

Her eyes went cool. "It's Tricia, isn't it?"

"Pardon me?"

"She told you what I said to her. About—"

"Stop. Please. Tricia didn't say a word to me about you except that she thinks you're very nice." *Nice.* "And she's right about that. It's just me. I'm sorry."

It took her a moment to respond. "Well, so am I, Noah. But at least you did prove me right about you. I haven't met many men who've had the class to deal with a relationship issue face-to-face. I appreciate it."

Although her words were civilized, her tone really wasn't. He didn't blame her. He never should've asked her out in the first place, had been reacting to his own frustration even after making a sensible plan. Yeah, he'd done some damage there. He wouldn't make that kind of mistake again.

When it came down to it, he was happy with the current status quo, especially if he could convince Tricia to stay. It was hard to believe that one woman could make such a difference in his life. *Their* lives.

One beautiful, sexy woman.

* * *

Tricia kept herself busy all evening. After dinner she supervised the children's packing of their suitcases to take to their grandparents' house the next day. Adam spent the least amount of time at it but packed the most, filling a second duffle bag with all his portable electronics.

"Where did our dad go tonight, Miss Tricia?" Zach asked as they had cookies and hot chocolate late in the evening.

"He told you. Out to dinner with a friend."

"Who?"

"You'll have to ask him that."

"Don't you know?"

Wasn't this a strange turn of events, Tricia thought. An interrogation. She might have expected it from Ashley, but not from Zach.

"You can ask him yourself, Zach."

"He's with Miss Cynthia," Zoe said, her words icy.

Stunned, Tricia took a bite of cookie, trying to look nonchalant. How did Zoe know that?

"Miss *Cynthia?*" Adam repeated, for once paying attention to the conversation. "You mean, like on a date?"

They all looked at Tricia. She raised her hands in surrender.

"That's stupid," Adam said. "If he wants to date somebody, it should be you. You're cool." He smiled and took a huge bite of cookie at the same time.

Tricia didn't know whether to laugh or cry. "Thank you for the compliment, Adam. I appreciate it."

"You're welcome. Can I go play a game?"

"Sure. Half an hour until bedtime, guys, okay? You've got to be up and on the road early."

They each carried their own mugs and napkins to the kitchen and took care of them, without her asking. She contemplated asking Zoe how she knew about Cynthia then decided against it, not wanting to give it too much significance.

Would one of them bring it up in the morning? Blindside Noah with it?

As soon as the kids were in bed and the house was quiet, she took a second mug of cocoa with her to her room. She changed into her bedtime T-shirt and pajama bottoms, turned on the television, found an old Cary Grant and Deborah Kerr movie she'd always loved, then snuggled into bed. But another couple took center screen in Tricia's mind.

Where were they now? Were they laughing over dessert? Holding hands across the table? Would he kiss her good-night?

This is ridiculous, she thought.

Tricia threw back the covers and went across the room. From the bookshelf she took down a photo album, a kind of life-summary album she'd put together recently, her own highlight reel, but in photographs. From the top of her dresser she grabbed a picture of Noah and the kids that she'd taken at the soccer party then printed on the computer.

She flipped through the album, stopping occasionally to recall a moment. One picture made her pause longer, a snapshot of her with Darrell as he was leaving for what became his last assignment. They'd been so young and so in love. She could look at him now and remember the fun they had and what he'd brought to her life, not the devastation of the loss. She'd clung to that loss for a lot longer than was healthy.

Tricia slid the Falcon family photo into a clear square at the back of the album. She ran her finger across it, smiling at the memory of the day. She loved those kids so much, even the belligerent Zoe, maybe even especially the belligerent Zoe, who was doing her best to be difficult, which only made Tricia love her more. She'd always rooted for the underdog.

Her finger landed on Noah. She ran it back and forth over his image, then stopped, her fingertip over his heart.

She loved *him,* too.

The revelation didn't come as a shout but a whisper, not as some flash of recognition but a sigh of acknowledgment. She'd been falling for him from the moment she watched him respond to his children come into his office when he and Tricia had been in negotiations. She'd seen strength of character there. Everything else had come slowly, day by day.

She was in love with him. And he was on a date.

She didn't want to leave, but staying meant she'd only have a family on loan until something changed—the kids grew up and went to college, or he fell in love and got married again.

Nor was she getting any younger. She didn't believe that love conquered all. Loving him was easy, but love itself was complicated and messy.

She shut the album, flattened her hands on it, bringing herself back to the present reality. What was wrong with her? She couldn't even think about staying. She'd made a commitment to her friend, who was counting on her. She was obligated for at least a year. By then the new teacher would be entrenched. Tricia couldn't even stay in touch. It would be unfair to the teacher, to all of them.

She needed to stop fantasizing about possibilities that didn't, couldn't exist. And really, it was a good thing she had somewhere else to go, something else to do. It was bound to save her from major heartbreak down the road.

Tricia heard a noise. She still hated the dark unknown of her surroundings. She crept to her door, opened it slightly...

Noah was home. She shut the door and picked up her watch from her dresser. Not even ten o'clock. Why was he back so early? A drive to Sacramento and back, plus dinner, should've taken at the very least an hour more.

She pressed her ear to her door, heard his shut, then absolute quiet descended on the house.

She had to see him. Tonight. She'd finally let herself accept that she loved him. She needed to see him, to see how it felt to look at him through new eyes.

Tricia pulled her flannel robe over her T-shirt and pajama bottoms, not bothering with slippers. She made her way down the hall and knocked lightly on his door.

He opened it as if he'd been standing there, waiting for her. His shirt was untucked and his shoes off. His hair looked like he'd run his hands through it a few times. Love swept through her, warming her, enveloping her.

"Everything okay?" he asked, ducking a little, capturing her gaze, pulling her out of her wonderment.

"I thought I should warn you," she said.

"Okay. About?"

"The kids know you went on a date with Cynthia. I don't know how, but they do."

"What was their reaction?"

She made herself smile. "Adam thought if you should be dating anyone, it should be me, because I'm cool."

He didn't smile at that. Big mistake sharing that bit of information, she decided.

"And the others?" he asked.

"Hard to say." She couldn't tell him how cold Zoe had been. That was something they had to work out themselves. "We were having cookies and hot chocolate, so they were busy with that. Anyway, I just wanted you to be forewarned, so you can figure out what you want to say to them."

"You think they'll ask?"

"Oh, yeah, they'll ask."

"Thanks. I appreciate the heads-up."

"Okay." Her hands found her pockets and plunged deep. "Good night." *I love you.*

"Tricia, I'd like to ask you something."

"Sure."

"Maybe you could come in for a few minutes? It seems ridiculous to have you stand in the hallway."

She'd never been in his bedroom before, had peeked in from the doorway but hadn't ever stepped inside. She did remember seeing a framed photograph of Margie on his dresser that wasn't there now. He'd put away the one in his office, too. She wanted to know what that meant.

He pointed to a sofa in a sitting area. She tightened her sash and sat, curling her legs and bare feet under her.

"Are you cold?" he asked, then without waiting for an answer, he picked up a remote and started the fireplace.

She shook her head.

"What?" he asked.

"This is something out of a James Bond movie to me. Gadgets galore. No more building a fire. Click. Instant heat." *Instant heat.* She wished she could get close enough to feel the heat she knew he radiated.

"If I had to build one, I'd rarely have one." He sat down. A few feet of space separated them. "If I'm being too personal, tell me. I'll understand."

"All right." She knew exactly what he was going to ask.

"Why are you a virgin?"

Bingo. "Because Darrell and I made a pledge to wait until our wedding night. Then he died, and I was in mourning for a very long time. Just about the time I was finding my place in the world again, my mother had the stroke, and I ended up quitting my job—and my life, in a way—to care for her. I let life-long friendships die. My world closed in. No one else came along who I wanted intimacy with. And that's it, in a nutshell."

"Do you regret it?"

"What? Not making love with Darrell?"

He nodded.

"Oh, yes. Biggest regret of my life. That, plus my parents dying so young, changed the way I look at life. My dad was only thirty-two, my mom barely fifty-three. My goal now, as I've said, is not to regret anything. I think it's why I'm able to take more risks than I used to, even though I seem to still need my safety net in place. I know that's a contradiction." She loved that they could sit and talk like, well, friends. They hadn't had a whole lot of relaxed conversation, she realized, that didn't pertain to the children.

He leaned an elbow on the back of the couch, angling toward her more, bringing a leg up so that he faced her directly. "Why were you crying?" he asked.

She linked her fingers in her lap. "While I was out for my drive, my Realtor called to say my house sold. It hit me kind of hard. Kind of like a guillotine cutting off all the years before, all the memories. I pretty much fell apart, right there on Main Street. Jake McCoy happened along right at that moment and let me cry on his shoulder."

"I'll bet he did."

She laughed. "I thought you'd decided to grow up and leave that feud behind."

"Yeah, well, I know Jake. Damsels in distress are his specialty."

"You sound jealous." She didn't dare let herself feel flattered.

He didn't say anything for a few seconds. "I just wish I'd been the one you turned to. My shoulder you cried on. You've taken care of all of us, Tricia. It would've felt good to take care of you in return."

She decided she didn't want to examine that. Or talk about

Jake anymore. He didn't matter. So she invited trouble instead. "How was your date?"

"I've been wondering if you would ask."

"When have I not interfered in your personal life?" she asked, which wasn't an entirely true statement. There was so much she wanted to know about him. Those horrible years with his father, and how he overcame it. The wonderful years with his wife. Tricia didn't have a bone of jealousy about Margie. She was glad he'd had a good marriage, and four beautiful children because of that marriage.

He nodded, all serious, except for sparkling eyes. "That's true. You are kind of in my face a lot."

"You need it."

"I'll reserve judgment on that."

She waited for him to answer as he stared across the room. And then she waited some more. "You don't have to tell me, of course," she said finally, uncomfortable with the silence.

"I didn't go on the date." He met her gaze. "I realized I wasn't ready. She was gracious."

Tricia didn't know how to react. Relief and joy swept through her that he hadn't held Cynthia's hand or kissed her good-night. On the other hand, he'd acknowledged anew that he was still grieving, still not ready for a woman in his life. His work and kids were enough.

"Do you think that's going to complicate your professional relationship with her now?" she asked, the only thing she could think of that wasn't too personal.

"Probably. I can live with it." He reached over and touched her hand. "This has been good. Thank you."

"Yes, it has." She stood. "I'm sure you need to get to bed. You'll be on the road for what, ten, twelve hours?"

He walked with her to the door. "I'll grab a couple hours of sleep before I head back."

"Would you call me when you get in? I'd like to know, you know, that you're home." Had she gone too far? That was a girlfriend kind of thing she was asking of him.

"You're going home, I take it."

"Yes, of course. No reason for me to be here, right?" She didn't expect an answer, so she hurried on. "I need to start boxing up my things. Having this week off is perfect timing for that."

He opened the door, held it as she passed by him. "Good night," she said. *I love you.*

"Sweet dreams," he answered.

But she didn't sleep, much less dream. After tossing and turning for an hour, she put her sneakers on and went outside. It seemed like the right time to conquer her worst fear.

Tricia grabbed a flashlight on her way out, then headed for the backyard. She didn't know if the noises she heard were real or her imagination, but she felt surrounded by sounds—dry leaves crackling, trees limbs creaking, fleeting footsteps. Her pulse thundered, her stomach churned. Still she remained planted in place.

A small animal zipped across the yard, twenty feet or so away. Dog? Cat? Fox? Large rat? Tricia didn't move. An owl startled her, taking off from a branch, its wings noisy. She ducked, but she didn't run.

She didn't know how long she stood there. Maybe fifteen minutes. Her bones were cold, her mind clear. Not that she wasn't afraid, but she could handle it now, not let it win, although she wouldn't walk beyond the buildings. She wasn't crazy. Then something approached from behind and nudged her. She jumped, raised her flashlight—

"Bear!" She exhaled the word on a relieved laugh as he shoved his muzzle against her hip, asking to be scratched. She dropped to her knees and accommodated him, relaxing more every second. Then he took off running, off to wherever he went next on his nightly route.

She hugged herself, looked up at the sky to see the stars she'd discovered her first night here. Then as she lowered her gaze she saw Noah framed in his bedroom window, watching her.

She smiled and waved, happy that she'd managed to tame some of her fear. He lifted a hand, left it on the window like a permanent greeting. It was too dark to see his face. She hoped he was smiling.

Her bed felt good this time, the down comforter creating warmth in short order. Peace descended on her. She could sleep now and dream of the man she loved.

Chapter Seventeen

Tricia's heartstrings were being tugged in four different directions by four wound-up, raring-to-go children at seven o'clock the next morning. Well, three raring-to-go children, anyway, Zoe having retreated into her own silent world. She'd started to scare Tricia with the intensity of her anger, or whatever it was. When they got back from their trip, Tricia would try to talk Noah into getting a counselor for her, since she didn't seem inclined to talk to either of them.

Tricia didn't want them to go, didn't want to spend a week apart from them. She had a hard time not telling them that.

Finally breakfast was done, the car packed. They were ready to go.

They gathered in the kitchen. "I hope you all have a wonderful time," she said, looking at each of them. "I love going to the beach, even in November."

Ashley gave her a big hug. Then Adam, who made it brief,

but who was grinning ear to ear. Zach came up next and squeezed her.

"Will you be here when we get back, Miss Tricia?"

"Yes, I will."

"Will you *always* be here?"

The world came to a halt. Tricia fired a look at Noah. How could she possibly answer that?

"Go ahead, Miss Tricia," Zoe said, harsh and cold. "Tell him you'll always be here. Lie to him. You're good at that."

"Zoe!" Ashley grabbed her sister by the arm and tried to pull her away.

"No. I'm sick of all the lies," Zoe said. "From you, too, *Father.*"

"Lies?" Adam repeated, looking back and forth between Noah and Tricia. "Who's lying?"

Zoe pointed at Tricia. "*She's* only going to be here until she moves away for another job. A *better* job." She angled her finger toward Noah then. "*He* knows it. Big, fat liars."

Tricia automatically reached for the angry girl. This was the burden she'd been carrying? Zoe wouldn't let her near. "I'm so sorry, Zoe. I—"

"Don't blame Miss Tricia," Noah interrupted, giving Tricia a look that said "I'm sorry" and "I'm in charge here" at the same time. "She wanted to tell you. It was my choice. My decision. There are reasons I didn't involve you, any of you. This is grown-up business."

"Oh, brother." Zoe threw up her hands. "Like you've been doing such a great job of being a grown-up. How many nannies have we had? How much time did you spend with us before Miss Tricia came and made you? What's going to happen when she leaves? Back to having no father again. What does that matter? You can't even tell the truth to your own children."

The other children had gone silent and still.

Tricia was handcuffed, unable to say or do anything. Noah had to handle it without interference.

"We *picked* her for you, me and Ashley," Zoe said, pounding her fist against her chest. "You promised you would be nice. But she's leaving anyway, aren't you, Miss Tricia? You're selling your house, and you're leaving."

She couldn't be anything less than honest. "Yes," she said.

"When?"

"I don't have an exact date. Maybe in a month." She dared a glance at Noah, who didn't look back.

"What do you mean you picked her for me?" Noah asked Zoe.

She let out a huge sigh. Ashley took over. "When we heard Miss Jessica tell someone on the phone that she was leaving, we talked to Uncle David. We asked him to find somebody good this time. Somebody who wouldn't go away just when we got them figured out. Somebody as old as you, Dad. You know, so she would be a friend, too. Uncle David found Miss Tricia. He said she could only take the job for a little while, but she was the best. He said everyone else was…" She looked to Zoe to fill in the blank.

"Frivolous," Zoe said.

"What does that mean?" Adam asked.

"Silly and stupid."

"Right," Ashley said. "Uncle David told us we had three months to get her to change her mind about her other job and stay with us." She put her arm around Zoe's waist. "We tried our best, Dad. And you promised to try. But it wasn't good enough."

"You're going away?" Zach asked Tricia, seeming to finally understand what was happening.

"I made a promise to someone, Zach. It's not like I have a choice. She's counting on me." She looked at Noah helplessly.

"*We're* counting on you!" Tears filled Zach's eyes. He looked accusingly at Noah, who had gone more rigid by the second—internalizing his emotions, Tricia figured. She wished he would just let go of them, open up. His children would not only understand but appreciate him for it.

"I have been trying to change her mind," Noah said. "Like you, I thought if I was nice enough, good enough, she would give up the other job and stay with us. But she has an obligation. Do you understand what that means, to have an obligation to someone?"

"We had her first," Zach said. "It's only fair."

"I made the commitment before I knew you," Tricia said, her heart breaking at their suffering. "I promise we'll find you someone wonderful. Your father's working on it. It'll be someone who can be here for you for a long time, someone you'll love."

"But I love *you*," Zach said. "I don't want to love someone else."

Silence hung thickly in the air until Noah took over. "Okay, everyone out to the car. We have to go."

A cheery goodbye was impossible now. They left with their heads down, shoulders slumped.

Noah held back after the door closed. "I guess we know what's bothering Zoe now," he said.

"Poor kid. I feel so guilty."

"Don't, Tricia. You're always willing to cut me a break. This time I don't deserve it. We both know it's my fault. I should have discussed this with them the moment I knew your plans. My fault. My problem. I'll fix it."

She wished she could hug him, kiss him goodbye. "Call me, please."

"Yeah."

She decided not to go outside to wave them off, afraid they wouldn't wave in return, which would hurt too much.

She guessed that having them know everything now would

bring about some changes. They wouldn't feel required to be nice to her—if that was what they had been doing all along—and they wouldn't hide their feelings. She admitted to wanting that honesty between them.

She also knew that it was going to be easier in some ways, too, since they had no expectation of her staying, although they would put distance between her and them, keep her at arm's length. The closeness they had would be a thing of the past. She was going to miss that more than she could say.

And then there was Noah. In her goal to keep her life safe and adventurous at the same time, things had gotten complicated—and yet simple.

She loved him, which was simple to do, complicated to undo, and not safe at all.

Noah glanced at his dashboard clock, saw it was close to ten-thirty. He was as tired as he could ever remember being. The drive itself had taken a lot out of him, but the emotional upheaval wore him out the most.

One good thing to come out of the day was that Zoe had finally purged herself of everything she'd been holding in. He'd taken her for a walk on the beach, and they'd sat and talked for more than an hour. All her fears had come spilling out—how much she missed her mother, how much she'd missed him when he wasn't around. How she worried about growing up and boys and the changes in her body and didn't know how to talk to him about it.

They talked about it, and everything else. He was as honest with her as he could be. At the end, she'd inched over and leaned against him. He'd put his arm around her, and she'd started to cry. His eyes had burned, too, hearing her sob. He finally pulled her into his lap and held her tight, her pretty hair, so like Margie's, smelling like strawberries.

The other good thing was an open discussion he had with the kids—about life in general and expectations in particular. It had become a full-blown brainstorming session, the longest, most productive family meeting they'd ever had.

As for Tricia, Zach had summed it up best when he'd said, "Well, she isn't gone yet!"

But Noah knew differently. He'd finally accepted that she had another obligation. That was that.

Noah was coming up to the freeway exit that would take him to Tricia's house. He had a couple of minutes to make up his mind, needed to settle on a plan. He did better with a plan, always had. When he acted hastily, like during that spontaneous liaison in his office with Tricia, it was disastrous.

So. A plan. He'd been thinking about it for most of the drive.

Option one: He could leave her alone for the week, not having any contact at all.

Option two: He could go see her now, even though he was exhausted and wouldn't be at his most logical.

Consequences of option one meant he wouldn't see her for a week. That wasn't an option.

Consequences of option two meant they could just talk, get things squared away, or they might make love.

Consequences of making love? Satisfaction…

He smiled at the understatement.

Other possible outcomes? Her first time. His first time in three years. He could end up being way too fast and she not enjoy it.

He laughed at that, knowing he was letting his concerns go a little far afield and was avoiding the real issues.

So. Real issues. He shows up at her place. She welcomes him. They end up in bed. It's great. Fabulous. Life-altering.

Then what? Do they agree to a week of sex? A week only? There didn't seem to be an option beyond that. A long-distance relationship had little chance of working. And a year from now, when she would be free to come back, another teacher would be in place. He couldn't do that to the children.

So, when are you going to put some value on yourself? Don't you deserve it?

Noah took the next exit and headed where he wanted to be most.

Wrapped in her robe, Tricia sat on her sofa, her legs tucked under her, the television off. She clung to her portable phone. It had been a very…long…day.

She should've been packing. Instead she'd been paralyzed. She had no safety net in this situation. She didn't know how the children felt. She didn't know how Noah felt. Being out of the loop had been slowly driving her out of her mind. She needed him to call, tell her what happened, what was going to happen now.

Headlights swept across her living room window, someone making a U-turn in front of her house. Then the sound of a car door shutting. Footsteps up her walkway.

She hurried to the door, looked out the peephole. Noah.

She waited for him to knock, giving herself a moment to collect herself, then opened the door.

He was framed in the doorway, an image captured in her mind as powerfully as a photograph. He presented her with a single yellow mum.

"You stole that from my neighbor's yard."

"In my defense, I tried to buy you roses. But it's Sunday night, so…"

She loved that he'd tried. "Come in."

"The house looks great," he said, looking around.

"Check out the kitchen. See how your handiwork came out."

He eyed her steadily and smiled. "Maybe later." He slipped his hand in his jacket pocket, pulled out something, handed it to her. A perfect little shell, orange and conical. "Zoe sent you this. She said to say she was sorry."

Tricia cradled it in her hand, then closed her fingers over it. Without a word she went into his arms, tears flowing fast and hot. "I was so scared they would hate me now."

He stroked her hair, her back, her arms. Soon, he wrapped her tighter, and let her cry herself out. Finally, he kissed her, tenderly, eloquently, if a kiss could be called that. It seemed to say more than words, anyway.

"We have a week," he said against her mouth.

She nodded. Her pulse picked up pace.

"You need to think about it," he said. "I have. It's what I want, even though I know it could complicate everything."

"I've *been* thinking about it. For weeks. It's what I want, too."

"Okay." He kissed her forehead, his breath rushing out against her skin. "One more gift." He dug into his jacket pocket again. "I couldn't find a place to sell me roses, but it was incredibly easy to find these."

He held up a package of condoms. She laughed, relaxing a little. "Brilliant minds think alike."

"You got some, too?"

She smiled. "I was hopeful."

"I know you're probably curious about what happened with the kids," he said. "But can I just sum it up and say everything is okay for now? We have more important things to do."

"Thank you for that." Happy, she took his hand and led him to her bedroom. She perched on the edge of the bed.

"I don't want to kiss you until we're both naked," he said. "If I kiss you now, I'll get tangled up in getting undressed. I want this to be slow and easy for you."

She reached for her sash. He stopped her. "I'd like to do that. Just give me a second to catch up to you."

She didn't mind a bit. Watching him undress was like a live-action Christmas present, her gift unwrapped a layer at a time. And, oh, what was underneath the packaging was rare, unique and memorable.

He took her hand, bringing her to her feet. "You're going to have to let me be in charge this first time," he said with a soft insistence. "Let me do the touching. Later, you can do whatever you want."

She didn't have any issues with his request except for wanting to touch him everywhere, to be close enough to him to taste his skin, and feel all the planes and ridges of his body. But then he untied her robe and let it fall to the floor, and her mind went blank—except for an awareness only of him. How he took a step back and looked at her, more than approval in his eyes—appreciation and arousal, too, although that was in full evidence already.

He pulled her in for a kiss, lips to lips, skin to skin, heart to heart. Heat to heat.

"I've wanted you for so long." He brushed his lips against hers again and again, her breathing more and more labored. "I dreamed about you, about this, but never expected it."

"Me, too. Exactly the same."

He took the kiss deep finally, groaned into her mouth. His tongue swirled, discovered, treasured. She savored the sounds and flavors of him, then he started on a slow path down her body, tempting her with lazy flicks, long strokes, intense explorations. She tipped her head back as he went lower still, his fingers busy, his mouth busier.

"You are a warrior woman," he said, kneeling. "Strong and smart and sexy."

His words upped the ante of arousal. She couldn't manage a single word in return, just threaded her fingers through his hair and pressed his scalp. Her strength disappeared as all her nerve endings seemed to narrow, gathering in one place. Her knees went weak. He moved her onto the bed, blanketed her body, settled between her legs, and kissed her long and deep and endlessly, urgency building, second by second.

She could hardly breathe. Her heart thundered so hard, she couldn't hear. Finally he nudged her legs apart. She'd waited for this moment for so long. So very long.

The tip of him felt scorching hot inside her as her body opened to his, welcoming him. He wasn't all the way inside her before the climax hit her full force, full measure, full glory. His mouth came down on hers, blocking the uncontrollable sounds bursting from her. He moved all the way up into her, bringing pressure that added to the eruption happening inside her, but no pain. No pain.

Then his body went rigid, moved more urgently, more rhythmically, and he followed her into the incredible oblivion that suspended time and sustained life.

Neither spoke, not for a long time, yet a sense of joy and satisfaction danced around them. She clung to him, treasured him, appreciated him.

"You are magnificent," she said finally.

He drew a deep, relaxed breath. "I bet you say that to all the guys."

She laughed and kissed him.

He rolled to his side, taking her along, tucking her close. "Do you need a blanket?" he asked.

"No. You're like a furnace."

"How are you?" His hands, his amazing hands, comforted, protected, soothed.

"Happy."

"No regrets?"

"No regrets at all. How about you?"

He sort of laughed, as if the idea was ridiculous. "No."

"How about tomorrow morning?"

"Ask me tomorrow," he said, teasing her, as he rubbed her back. "Thank you. I know it was a gift."

"I'm glad it was you."

He yawned and closed his eyes. Sleep came instantly. She wasn't surprised, considering the day he'd had.

She figured she'd give him a few hours, then take him at his word that she could do whatever she wanted to him.

She mentally rubbed her hands together. She had a lot of years to catch up on. Oh, yeah. He would never know what hit him.

Chapter Eighteen

Nerves wrapped around Tricia like a boa constrictor, slithering and squeezing. It was Sunday. She hadn't seen the children in a week. They were due home with Noah at any minute. She had no idea how they were going to react to her.

And she didn't know how she was going to stand not sleeping with him, hadn't truly understood how hard it was going to be to give him up. He'd spent the workweek at her house, then they'd come back to his house Friday night. There were a number of rooms that held fond memories for her.

She smiled at the thought, especially about the time she'd cleared his desktop and had her way with him, a fantasy come true—except she'd had to help him sort out his papers afterward, which he made her do naked.

Yes, memories. Great memories. Ones that had to sustain her.

That morning, before he left for San Luis Obispo, he told her he'd been in touch with Denise to start the search process for a new teacher. The kids had given him a list of what they wanted. He'd promised them they could be involved in the hiring. They were not just a family now, but a team.

He didn't shy away from talking honestly about his relationship with Tricia, either. That this was the end of it, this morning, in his big bed with the view of forested hills and the glorious sunrise.

She got it. She'd gotten it since he'd come home from his nondate with Cynthia. He wasn't ready to date, but an affair worked for him.

She had no right to be angry about that. He'd been honest from the beginning. A week only. Fantasies fulfilled. Questions answered. Curiosities satisfied. They couldn't let on to the children that anything was different.

So why was she angry? Anger was unfamiliar territory. It generally took a lot to rile her.

She acknowledged the worst of it—she'd hoped he would fall in love with her. And while the sex was great, and the conversations amazing and endless, it hadn't happened for him. She'd wanted him to come to a big revelation and wake up this morning, their last morning, and tell her he loved her. It hadn't happened. He just talked of being careful, of not letting on there was anything between them.

And if he'd said he loved you? What then?

She would've found a way to deal with the other job. No question about it.

She saw the car approach. A chunk of hot lead lodged in her stomach. Should she go outside to greet them?

She stayed put. Before too long the door opened. Adam popped in, a duffle bag in each hand.

"Yo," he said with a toss of his head.

"How are you?" she asked, nerves hitting her hard. *I missed you. I missed you so much....*

"Pretty good." He kept moving.

Ashley followed. She smiled, but it wasn't her sparkling-eyes, flashing-teeth smile of the past. And she didn't hug Tricia. "Hi, Miss Tricia," she said as she walked through.

"Did you have a good time?" *I missed you....*

"Yes. My grandparents are a lot of fun." Then she was gone.

Zach came in, struggling with a suitcase way too big for him. He didn't hug her, either, which hurt more than with the others. Should she call in his marker and ask for one of those hugs he said he had plenty of? No. She couldn't force the issue. It would only make things harder.

"How was the ocean?" she asked. *I missed you....*

"Kinda cold. And a wave knocked me down. It hurt, and I got sand in my underwear."

She wanted to talk to him some more but he kept going.

Zoe finally walked in. She stood in the doorway staring at Tricia.

"I missed you," Tricia said without stopping to think about it.

Zoe dropped her bag and threw herself into Tricia's arms. "I missed you, too."

"Thank you for the shell, Zoe. It's the most special present anyone has ever given me."

"I'm sorry, Miss Tricia. Did my dad tell you?"

"Yes." Tricia looked up as Noah joined them. He smiled at her, then his gaze went all tender as he looked at Zoe. "You don't have anything to be sorry about, sweetie. I understood completely. I'm sorry, too."

Tricia wanted to pull Noah into the hug, too. Group hug, she wanted to shout, and have all of them come running, entwining arms and bodies until they laughed.

Zoe's face shone when she looked up at Tricia. Then she took off at top speed.

Noah took a couple of steps, stopping short of her.

"Looks like everyone had a good time," she said, linking her fingers.

"Yes. The week apart was a good way to start fresh, all of us. I feel like I've been given a new life."

"That's wonderful, Noah."

He came closer, close enough to touch, but he didn't. "It's all because of you."

"No. You would've found your way—"

"It's all because of you, Tricia. We'll never forget you. None of us."

She laughed nervously. "No need to throw me a farewell party yet."

His smile was bittersweet. "I'm going to check on them, then go to bed."

"Should I tuck them in, too, do you think? I'm at a loss here."

"I think you should do what feels right. They may not be quite as open or receptive as they were. Just so you're prepared."

Zoe will be, though. And that was a triumph in itself.

Noah lay in bed that night trying to sleep. He should have been exhausted. Hell, he *was* exhausted. The drive alone was enough to be its own kind of sleep aid. Factor in he was sleeping alone for the first time in seven days, and it changed everything.

He missed her. Missed the feel of her in his arms. The sound of her voice as they talked well into the night. Her playfulness when they showered together, her body sleek with soap. It had been a long time since he'd laughed so much, if he'd ever laughed so much.

When he stretched out his arm now, he felt only a cool sheet over a flat mattress, not a warm, curvy body that molded to his. She'd greeted him at the front door every night after work like he was the only man on earth.

Like she loved him.

But if she loved him, she would've said so. Or figured out a way to stay with them instead of taking the other job. She didn't offer to do that. She didn't say she loved him.

He hadn't set out to seduce her into staying, but during their week together, he'd seen it as a possibility.

But she never had. She had an obligation. He wouldn't have admired her as much if she didn't take her commitments seriously. He'd tried to make sure the children understood that as they talked during the drive home, using the example as a way of getting them to see the importance of keeping your word. It was a good life lesson, he'd decided, even if the outcome wasn't the desired one.

The kids adjusted easier than he'd expected, almost shrugging it off.

Which led him to believe they had a plan.

Noah had no intention of interfering. If his only chance for success was a little deviousness from his children, who was he to spoil their fun? What had Tricia told him her mantra was? *Life is short. Make it an adventure.*

Maybe there was still a chance.

Chapter Nineteen

November gave up its amber glow to the blues and whites of early December morning frosts. Tricia had started getting up earlier in the morning and going for a walk, watching her breath cloud around her, the chill biting, invigorating, renewing. She tried not to think so hard while she walked but just enjoy the beauty. Before too long, escrow would close on her house. She had assumed she would leave Noah's house at the same time, when the moving van was loaded and gone.

There was a hitch in the plans, however. No new teacher was in place yet.

It wasn't like they hadn't been looking. They'd interviewed several applicants. No one was right. They were too old, too young, too strict, too lenient. One liked bending the rules. Another enforced every one. Balance. They were missing balance.

Then the inevitable day when Ms. Right came along, or

rather Ms. Megan Wright. When she came to the door for her interview, Tricia thought she was looking in a mirror. Well, okay, maybe not *that* close a match, but an uncanny one. She was as tall, as blond, as friendly. Competent, progressive, forward-thinking. Fun. And she was willing to live in 24/7.

They held a family meeting after she left, then Noah tracked Tricia down and told her the offer would be made tomorrow. Tricia was free to leave.

Time to pull up roots.

She thought she saw a bit of sympathy in his eyes after he delivered the news. They'd danced around each other for two weeks, surrounded by crystal-clear memories of the week of exquisite intimacy they'd shared, in and out of bed. She'd come so close so many times to knocking on his door in the middle of the night. And she'd seen the hunger in his eyes for her, too— and the restraint.

Evenings were the hardest, when she met with him in his office to report on the day with the children. He'd kept the desk between them, had never once alluded to their relationship.

As for the children, they were different, too, but in a wonderful way. They were sweet to her and to each other, but they bickered a little more, which she saw as healthy. They didn't let things build up to a breaking point. A normal household with a loving father and four well-loved children, learning how to function well in the world later because of what they learned about relationships at home.

And tomorrow someone else would take her place, and be well loved by these beautiful children.

Would she be Ms. Wright for Noah, too?

"I think this is the longest you've gone without speaking," he said, having waited for her to respond.

She didn't know what to say. "I'm sorry."

"It's what you wanted, right?"

No. But she nodded. "You expect she'll accept the job offer?"

"According to Denise, yes."

He seemed to be waiting for something. "She seems great," she said. "The kids took to her right away." *Did you, too?* she wanted to ask.

"It's good that they were part of the process this time. Should make for a smooth transition."

"That's important."

"Yes."

He still seemed to be waiting for something. *What do you want, Noah?*

A few more seconds passed without conversation. "I'm going to join the kids in the family room," he said. "Want to come along?"

No. She needed to go somewhere and cry. It hit her so hard, she couldn't wait to get away.

Zach came into the living room and tugged on her sweater. "Miss Tricia?"

She swallowed the lump in her throat, set a hand on his shoulder. "Yes, Zachary?"

He placed a DVD in her hands. "Would you watch this with me?"

It was the video of his mother, the one he hadn't wanted to watch before.

She looked at Noah, who gave nothing away with his expression. Why wasn't he offering to watch it with his son?

Because Zach asked you. She could hear the words as clearly as if he'd said them aloud.

"Of course I would, Zach. Where should we go?" They couldn't use the family room, since everyone else was there.

"How about my room?" Noah said. "Would you like that, Zach?"

He nodded.

"Why don't you head up there?" Tricia said. "I'll be right behind you."

He trooped up the stairs. Tricia looked at Noah. "What's going on?"

"No idea."

"Are you okay with me doing this with him? Would you rather I talk him into letting you be there, instead—or both of us?"

"He wants you. I don't want to interfere with that, not about something this emotional. I guess the question is, are *you* okay with it?"

"Honestly? I've been curious about her."

His brows raised a little. "Question answered, then."

Oh, she wanted to kiss him. Hold him. Sleep curled against him. Wake to his handsome face in the morning and see his sleepy, sexy smile. She gave in to the ache for just a moment, put her hand on his chest and looked into his eyes. She saw the same temptation reflected back, his breath catching a little. She loved this man completely, infinitely.

"See you later," she said, hoping he would come to her after the children were asleep, for one last time.

Zach had the DVD in the machine when she got there. He'd pulled back the covers, piled pillows against the headboard and was stretched out there, the remote in hand. She climbed in bed with him, remembered the two nights she'd spent there in Noah's arms.

Zach snuggled close. Taking her cue from him, she put an arm around him, understanding that he needed her to be close, to feel emotionally safe. He started the video.

It was a professionally put together disc, set to music, with photographs of Margie as a baby, a child, a teenager, a college student, a bride. Twins in her arms. Another two babies later, with toddlers around her, too. Noah, looking tentative holding the girls, and then comfortable with the boys. Like Ashley,

Margie smiled a lot, obviously adored her children and her husband. Every image proved it.

There were snippets from their vacations in Disneyland and Disney World. Birthday parties. Halloweens. Christmases. Joyful times.

Zach didn't move, didn't comment. Occasionally he squeezed Tricia's hand, but that was all. Then when it was over, he was quiet for quite a while before he finally spoke.

"She sure loved us."

Tricia gathered him closer. "Oh, sweetie. She sure did."

"I love you, Miss Tricia," he whispered.

"I love you, too. So much."

"I don't want you to go."

Noah came into the room and saw them hugging. He walked toward them. She pressed her fingers to the corners of her eyes, trying to staunch a fresh flow of tears. Zach popped up, ran across the bed and leaped into Noah's arms. Tricia couldn't bear the tender scene. She hurried out of the room and went to her own.

Her own—for one more night.

Then after staring at her phone for a few long seconds, she picked it up and dialed.

Noah lay in his bed, the dark surrounding him, the scent of Tricia's perfume on his pillow. He'd been waiting two weeks for her to come to him, had slept fitfully every night, anticipation always on his mind. She never came. He never went to her. He knew that neither of them needed that complication, but it hadn't stopped him from hoping.

Now that they'd found a new teacher, she would leave. As early as tomorrow. Should he—could he—go to her tonight? Should he wait until she went back to Sacramento and see then if she wanted to continue what they'd started? They would have only until she left town.

Left town. Left their lives. His life.

He pushed himself up, his knees raised, his head tipped back, resting against the headboard.

The thought of her being gone from his life hit him like a gut punch, hard and out of the blue. Staggering. His hope that the kids had a plan hadn't turned out to be true. They hadn't interfered in the hiring process, hadn't delayed anything. And when a qualified person showed up today, they'd expressed their approval.

Weren't children supposed to be difficult when they weren't getting their way? He knew they wanted Tricia to stay.

He dragged the pillow she'd rested against earlier to press into his face, inhaling her scent, wishing for her, conjuring her up.

A quiet knock came at his door, then it opened just a crack.

"Noah?" she whispered.

"Come in," he said in a hurry. Was that all it took? Wishing for her? He reached over, turned on a bedside lamp, saw she was still dressed—at two in the morning.

"I'm sorry to bother you," she said.

He shook his head, not sure what to say until he knew why she was there. He patted the bed, inviting her to sit.

"I have to talk to you about something," she began, then stopped to take a breath, her hand pressed to her stomach.

"You're pregnant?" he asked, setting his hand on hers, waiting for the panic that should come but didn't.

"I— Pregnant?" She frowned. "No. Why would you think— Never mind. Here's the thing. I called my friend tonight, the one whose job I'm taking. I told her I couldn't take the job after all. She'd have to find someone else."

Couldn't do it? Wasn't leaving? "You backed out of the job? Out of your commitment?"

"What else could I do? I can't let just anyone teach your children. And, you know, the more I think about that Megan Wright, the more I think she's too good to be true."

He tried not to smile. If he wasn't mistaken, Miss Tricia was a little bit jealous. "I trust your instincts," he said. "If you don't think she's right, then we should rethink it."

"There's no rethinking about it. I'm staying. You have to keep me, because now I don't have a house or a job."

"I have to? Who's the boss here?"

"Technically, you are."

"Technically?"

She shrugged. He didn't buy the nonchalant act for a minute. "What did your friend say when you told her?"

"This is the funny part. She's been trying to figure out a way to tell me that her husband lost his job, and they decided he should be Mr. Mom for now. The school is offering me a teaching position, but I don't want it. I have a job here, a job I love."

A new kind of hope caught fire inside Noah, breaking down the wall he'd put up in order to survive her leaving. Because there were no barriers now, he heard something in her voice he hadn't heard before, or maybe she hadn't allowed him to hear it before. "There's going to be a problem with your plan," he said.

"You haven't offered her the job yet. You wouldn't have to renege."

He heard a bit of panic in her voice. It settled him like nothing else could have. He reached for her hands, feeling confident, and finally understood his jumbled emotions and sleepless nights.

"But, you see, Tricia, I can't continue to stay in the same house with you," he said, feeling her try to pull away, "and not be with you, in every sense of the word. You see, I've fallen in love with you."

After a moment, she threw herself into his arms, knocking him against the headboard. "I love you, too. Oh, Noah. I love you so much."

"You're not going to cry, are you?"

"I might." Her words were muffled by his shoulder. "Deal with it."

He laughed, and then he kissed her, tenderly at first, desperately after a minute. "I've missed you," he said.

"Not anywhere near as much as I've missed you."

"Well, we could spend a little time arguing about that, or I could go lock the door. You want to argue about that?"

"Who, me? Argue? Never."

By the time he'd walked to the door and back, she'd stripped and was kneeling in the middle of his bed waiting. He knelt in front of her. "I know this is fast. David's going to ride the hell out of me. But, here goes. I love you with all my heart. Will you marry me?"

She framed his face with her hands. "Yes."

"I hope you like children," he said with a grin.

She grinned back. "Pretty well, I guess. You know where I can get a couple of matched sets?"

Would she want more than that? A child with him? "Do you, that is, having more children, is it—"

"Yes," she said instantly. "One or two, if you're in agreement."

"Yes. Just not quadruplets, please." He kissed her, grateful and happy. "I've wondered for a long time if I would, or could, find someone who would love my children as if they were her own. I know you do. You were willing to stay on here, just as their teacher, weren't you? Without any promise from me? No declaration of love."

"Yes, although to be honest, it may have ended up being harder than I expected, being here, not being with you. In the end, the question I asked myself was, would I be happier with you or without you? I made my decision."

They fell into each other, made love this time knowing they loved, then slept a little while before she returned to her room, glowing and excited. In the morning they gathered the children in the family room.

"I have news," Noah said, eyeing each curious face. "I've asked Miss Tricia to marry me, and she said yes."

There was a long moment of silence, then smiles began to appear on their faces.

"It worked!" Adam shouted, jumping up. Zach did, too, high-fiving him.

Zoe and Ashley hugged.

"What worked?" Noah asked, glancing at Tricia, who shrugged.

"Our plan," Zach said, obviously proud of himself.

"I'm afraid to ask." So he'd been right. It made him happy to know he knew his children that well. He wouldn't let on to them, however. Not now, not ever. "What plan would that be, my plotting children?"

"We talked to Denise," Zoe said, "and told her to send a whole lot of people we wouldn't like, figuring Miss Tricia would get upset and say okay, okay, she'll stay. But that didn't work. So then Uncle David said, what if he sent someone that we all could say we liked. He bet Miss Tricia would be jealous and come to her senses."

"You mean if I offered Ms. Wright the job today, she would have declined?" Noah asked.

"She's got a job already," Ashley said, grinning. "She's big shot vice president of a bank or something. But she looks like Miss Tricia, and Uncle David said Miss Tricia wouldn't like that."

Tricia gasped, then started laughing, then bent over, she was laughing so hard. "Why you devious children," she said finally. "And can I say, I love Uncle David."

"We didn't want you to go," Adam said, a big admission for him.

"And now you can kind of be our mom," Zach said, coming up to her.

"I think Mom would be okay with that," Ashley said, looking at Noah.

"I think you're right. We won't ever forget her, I promise you."

Tricia was fighting tears. "When I first came here, I thought you all needed me. But the truth is, *I* needed all of you. And I sure could use one of those hugs now, if you don't mind," she said to Zach, opening her arms. He went straight into them. Pretty soon the others pushed their way in, bringing Noah into the circle as well.

He looked into Tricia's eyes over his children's heads. She looked back, her eyes shimmering, love shining from her, a beacon that lit up the whole room. He didn't know how he'd gotten lucky twice in his life. Maybe he was being rewarded for having survived childhood. Who knew?

All he knew for sure was that he was a happy man.

* * * * *

Don't miss Gideon's story,
THE MILLIONAIRE'S CHRISTMAS WIFE,
on sale in November
from Silhouette Special Edition.

Here's a sneak peek at
THE CEO'S CHRISTMAS PROPOSITION,
the first in USA TODAY *bestselling author*
Merline Lovelace's HOLIDAYS ABROAD *trilogy*
coming in November 2008.

American Devon McShay is about to get the Christmas surprise of a lifetime when she meets her new client, sexy billionaire Caleb Logan, for the very first time.

Silhouette *Desire*

Available November 20

Her breath whistled out in a sigh of relief when he exited Customs. Devon recognized him right away from the newspaper and magazine articles her friend and partner Sabrina had looked up during her frantic prep work.

Caleb John Logan, Jr. Thirty-one. Six-two. With jet-black hair, laser-blue eyes and a linebacker's shoulders under his charcoal-gray cashmere overcoat. His jaw-dropping good looks didn't score him any points with Devon. She'd learned the hard way not to trust handsome heartbreakers like Cal Logan.

But he was a client. An important one. And she was willing to give someone who'd served a hitch in the marines before earning a B.S. from the University of Oregon, an MBA from Stanford and his first million at the ripe old age of twenty-six the benefit of the doubt.

Right up until he spotted the hot-pink pashmina, that is.

Devon knew the flash of color was more visible than the sign she held up with his name on it. So she wasn't surprised when Logan picked her out of the crowd and cut in her direction. She'd just plastered on her best businesswoman smile when he whipped an arm around her waist. The next moment she was sprawled against his cashmere-covered chest.

"Hello, brown eyes."

Swooping down, he covered her mouth with his.

Sheer astonishment kept Devon rooted to the spot for a few seconds while her mind whirled chaotically. Her first thought was that her client had downed a few too many drinks during the long flight. Her second, that he'd mistaken the kind of escort and consulting services her company provided. Her third shoved everything else out of her head.

The man could kiss!

His mouth moved over hers with a skill that ignited sparks at a half dozen flash points throughout her body. Devon hadn't experienced that kind of spontaneous combustion in a while. A *long* while.

The sparks were still popping when she pushed off his chest, only now they fueled a flush of anger.

"Do you always greet women you don't know with a lip-lock, Mr. Logan?"

A smile crinkled the skin at the corners of his eyes. "As a matter of fact, I don't. That was from Don."

"Huh?"

"He said he owed you one from New Year's Eve two years ago and made me promise to deliver it."

She stared up at him in total incomprehension. Logan hooked a brow and attempted to prompt a nonexistent memory.

"He abandoned you at the Waldorf. Five minutes before midnight. To deliver twins."

"I don't have a clue who or what you're…"

Understanding burst like a water balloon.

"Wait a sec. Are you talking about Sabrina's old boyfriend? Your buddy, who's now an ob-gyn doc?"

It was Logan's turn to look startled. He recovered faster than Devon had, though. His smile widened into a rueful grin.

"I take it you're not Sabrina Russo."

"No, Mr. Logan, I am *not*."

* * * * *

Be sure to look for
THE CEO'S CHRISTMAS PROPOSITION
by Merline Lovelace.
Available in November 2008
wherever books are sold,
including most bookstores, supermarkets,
drugstores and discount stores.

MARRIED BY CHRISTMAS

Playboy billionaire Elijah Vanaldi has discovered
he is guardian to his small orphaned nephew.
But his reputation makes some people question
his ability to be a father. He knows he must
fight to protect the child, and he'll do anything
it takes. Ainslie Farrell is jobless, homeless and
desperate—and when Elijah offers her a position
in his household she simply can't refuse....

Available in November

HIRED: THE ITALIAN'S CONVENIENT MISTRESS

by

CAROL MARINELLI

Book #29

nocturne™

**ESCAPE THE CHILL OF WINTER WITH TWO SPECIAL
STORIES FROM BESTSELLING AUTHORS**

MICHELE
HAUF

AND

VIVI ANNA

WINTER KISSED

In "A Kiss of Frost," photographer Kate Wilson experiences
the icy kisses of Jal Frosti, but soon learns that this icy god
has a deadly ulterior motive. Can Kate's love melt his heart?

In "Ice Bound," Dr. Darien Calder travels to the north
island of Japan, where he discovers an icy goddess who is
rumored to freeze doomed travelers. Darien is determined
to melt her beautiful but frosty exterior and break her of
the curse she carries...before it's too late.

Available November wherever books are sold.

www.eHarlequin.com
www.paranormalromanceblog.wordpress.com
SN61799

REQUEST YOUR FREE BOOKS!
2 FREE NOVELS PLUS 2 FREE GIFTS!

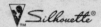

SPECIAL EDITION®
Life, Love and Family!

YES! Please send me 2 FREE Silhouette Special Edition® novels and my 2 FREE gifts (gifts are worth about $10). After receiving them, if I don't wish to receive any more books, I can return the shipping statement marked "cancel." If I don't cancel, I will receive 6 brand-new novels every month and be billed just $4.24 per book in the U.S. or $4.99 per book in Canada, plus 25¢ shipping and handling per book and applicable taxes, if any*. That's a savings of at least 15% off the cover price! I understand that accepting the 2 free books and gifts places me under no obligation to buy anything. I can always return a shipment and cancel at any time. Even if I never buy another book from Silhouette, the two free books and gifts are mine to keep forever.

235 SDN EEYU   335 SDN EEY6

Name _____ (PLEASE PRINT)

Address _____ Apt. #

City _____ State/Prov. _____ Zip/Postal Code

Signature (if under 18, a parent or guardian must sign)

Mail to the **Silhouette Reader Service:**
IN U.S.A.: P.O. Box 1867, Buffalo, NY 14240-1867
IN CANADA: P.O. Box 609, Fort Erie, Ontario L2A 5X3

Not valid to current subscribers of Silhouette Special Edition books.

Want to try two free books from another line?
Call 1-800-873-8635 or visit www.morefreebooks.com.

* Terms and prices subject to change without notice. N.Y. residents add applicable sales tax. Canadian residents will be charged applicable provincial taxes and GST. Offer not valid in Quebec. This offer is limited to one order per household. All orders subject to approval. Credit or debit balances in a customer's account(s) may be offset by any other outstanding balance owed by or to the customer. Please allow 4 to 6 weeks for delivery. Offer available while quantities last.

Your Privacy: Silhouette is committed to protecting your privacy. Our Privacy Policy is available online at www.eHarlequin.com or upon request from the Reader Service. From time to time we make our lists of customers available to reputable third parties who may have a product or service of interest to you. If you would prefer we not share your name and address, please check here. ☐

Inside ROMANCE

Stay up-to-date on all your romance reading news!

The Inside Romance newsletter is a FREE quarterly newsletter highlighting our upcoming series releases and promotions!

Click on the <u>Inside Romance</u> link on the front page of **www.eHarlequin.com** or e-mail us at insideromance@harlequin.ca to sign up to receive your FREE newsletter today!

You can also subscribe by writing us at: HARLEQUIN BOOKS Attention: Customer Service Department P.O. Box 9057, Buffalo, NY 14269-9057

Please allow 4-6 weeks for delivery of the first issue by mail.

COMING NEXT MONTH

SSECNM1008BPA